“Are you ready to

“I don’t think my horse wants to race yours,” said Major. “He agrees that a lady should remain a lady.”

“I am a lady—a lady of the prairie. Not one of your cosseted plantation debutantes, but a lady nonetheless.”

That annoyed him—mostly because he knew some of the “cosseted plantation debutantes” she spoke of, and she was right on the mark. They always bored him to tears—one reason he was yet unwed. “And what, pray tell, does a ‘lady of the prairie’ do when she races like a madwoman?”

“She wins, of course!” She gave a low whistle, causing her horse to prance around.

“Here now, what do you think you’re doing?”

“Getting ready. Are you?”

“Confound it, woman, will you get the notion of racing out of your head?”

“No, I won’t. Besides, the horses want to.”

“I don’t care what the horses want!”

“What’s the matter, Mr. Comfort? Are you afraid you’ll lose…” she leaned slightly toward him “…to a girl?”

Kit Morgan has written all her life. Her whimsical stories are fun, inspirational, sweet and clean, and depict a strong sense of family and community. She was raised by a homicide detective, so one would think she'd write suspense, but no. Kit likes fun and romantic Westerns! Kit resides in the beautiful Pacific Northwest in a little log cabin on Clear Creek, after which her fictional town that appears in many of her books is named.

Dear Mr. Comfort

KIT MORGAN

If you purchased this book without a cover you should be aware that this book is stolen property. It was reported as "unsold and destroyed" to the publisher, and neither the author nor the publisher has received any payment for this "stripped book."

Recycling programs for this product may not exist in your area.

ISBN-13: 978-1-335-08023-3

Dear Mr. Comfort

First published in 2016 by Kit Morgan.
This edition published in 2020.

Copyright © 2016 by Kit Morgan

All rights reserved. No part of this book may be used or reproduced in any manner whatsoever without written permission except in the case of brief quotations embodied in critical articles and reviews.

This is a work of fiction. Names, characters, places and incidents are either the product of the author's imagination or are used fictitiously. Any resemblance to actual persons, living or dead, businesses, companies, events or locales is entirely coincidental.

This edition published by arrangement with Harlequin Books S.A.

For questions and comments about the quality of this book, please contact us at CustomerService@Harlequin.com.

Harlequin Enterprises ULC
22 Adelaide St. West, 40th Floor
Toronto, Ontario M5H 4E3, Canada
www.Harlequin.com

Printed in U.S.A.

Dear Mr. Comfort

Prologue

Denver, Colorado, 1901

Fantine Le Blanc stared in stunned silence at her eccentric employer.

Mrs. Adelia Pettigrew placed her silver monocle over one eye, studying Fantine as one would some rare animal species. "Have you all your faculties, *ma belle*?"

Fantine started at the question. "*Oui, Madame* Pettigrew. Of course." Except that Mrs. Pettigrew had just told her the most fantastic tale, one that left poor Fantine in suspense. She had to know more about the Comfort family—six brothers and a sister who due to extraordinary circumstances had come west from Savannah, Georgia to the little town of Clear Creek, Oregon.

The basics were simple enough. The sister, Pleasant, had become one of Mrs. Pettigrew's mail-order brides and married a local. Her brothers had tracked her down, intending to bring her back home, but settled in Clear Creek instead. It was the details, the lunatic assortment of details, which had left Fantine in shock. "So what happened?" she asked in exasperation.

Mrs. Pettigrew's brows knitted. "I just told you what happened, *ma douce*."

"But surely there must be more! What did the brothers do? How did they live?"

"The men's camp, of course, just as I told you. For Heaven's sake, Fantine, didn't you listen?"

"*Oui, oui.* But that is why I am asking—what happened *after*?"

Mrs. Pettigrew straightened and looked at her pocket watch. They were seated on cushions on the floor around a low table, with at least half a dozen dogs—plus a few others roaming the room or scratching at the French doors, wanting out. Who knew whom they belonged to, but Mrs. Pettigrew took tea with them most afternoons. It was one of her many eccentricities that made her mildly infamous in Denver society. "Oh dear, look at the time!"

Fantine glanced at the clock on the wall. 5:30. "Tea is over then?"

"Of course it is," Mrs. Pettigrew said with a quick roll of the eyes. "And time for our guests to be getting home."

Fantine struggled up off her cushion, went to the doors and, having learned from past experience, got out of the way. The dogs raced for it, bumping and shoving their way to freedom and home. "*Jusqu'á demain, mes amis!*" Mrs. Pettigrew called after them with a wave, then, when the last one had departed, glanced at Fantine. "Well don't just stand there, *ma petite*—close the blasted door!"

Fantine noticed that for a moment, Mrs. Pettigrew's French accent shifted to deep-Southern. She fought the urge to laugh, fully aware that unlike her own, her employer's accent was fake. But she kept quiet about such things. She needed the job more than she needed to gossip.

Besides, Fantine liked her. Mrs. Pettigrew's fantastic stories of her clients fascinated her, and brought an odd joy to her unusual position as the lady's assistant. She might be halfway round the bend, but she was kind, generous, and one of the wealthiest women—if not the wealthiest—in Colorado. So what if she wore a bright pink gown and a tiara just to take tea with a bunch of silly pooches? There were far worse vices.

But enough of that. "The Comfort brothers, *madame*?" Fantine prompted. "You will tell me what happened to them?"

"Oh yes, the brothers." She held out a hand. "Help me up, will you?"

Fantine rushed to her side and pulled the woman to her feet. "What happened to Major? Did you send him a mail-order bride?"

"Ah, yes. Major Quincy Comfort, the eldest. I did send him a bride, come to think of it, but in a rather...*qu'est-ce que c'est*...roundabout way? Things didn't go as I would have wished, but they turned out well—eventually. No one got hurt too badly, as I recall..."

"Hurt? Who was hurt?"

Mrs. Pettigrew waved her concerns away. "No, you misunderstand...well, perhaps you don't. No one actually *died*..."

"Died?!"

"Sorry—poor choice of words..."

"What happened?" Fantine asked. "Is there a letter?"

"Oh yes, of course." Mrs. Pettigrew's eyes flicked toward her office down the hall.

"Shall I fetch it for you?"

"No need, *ma belle*—I'll get it myself." She left the sitting room and went straight to her office, Fantine on her heels. "Now, where did I put it?" she mused, looking over the multitude of framed letters that covered the room like patchy wallpaper.

Fantine felt her heart sink. What if the woman couldn't find it? She hadn't had enough time to study all the letters—she was always too busy—but when she did have a moment, she liked to read a few. "Can I help?"

"No, no—this particular letter is, how you say, unique. Really, I should say *letters*—I keep them all together in one frame. Though perhaps I should not—they are by different people. But there's only so much room on the walls..."

"How many?" Fantine interrupted.

Mrs. Pettigrew shrugged. "Four, five? Maybe more I forget."

"Why so many?"

"Aha—there they are!" Mrs. Pettigrew had stopped at the far wall, and was looking up near the ceiling.

Fantine joined her. "Which one is it?"

"Second from the left at the very top. The one with the royal seal."

"Royal seal?"

"*Oui*."

Fantine, now more curious than ever, quickly scanned the room for something to stand on, but found nothing tall enough. That explained the layer of dust on the top few rows. "Do we have a ladder?"

"Hmmm...somewhere," Mrs. Pettigrew mused. "In the carriage house, I believe."

Fantine felt her heart sink. No wonder her employer had never made her dust the top ones. There wasn't a convenient way to. But what else could she do? "I will get it right away," she sighed, bobbing a curtsy.

"Don't be silly, you'll break your neck. These are twelve-foot walls, *ma petite*." Mrs. Pettigrew waved to the door. "That's what we have Mr. Tugs for."

"The gardener?!" Fantine cried. "But, *madame*, he is so...so old! He should not climb a ladder!"

"You underestimate him, *ma cherie*. He was once an acrobat with the famous Clarke circus in London—traveled with them for many years."

Fantine could only stare. Mr. Tugs an acrobat? She'd suspected Tugs was a nickname—he could usually be found tugging on the rose bushes and shrubbery, claiming it was good exercise for the plants. Perhaps it was really a stage name. Nonetheless, he had to be over eighty years old. "What if he were to fall?"

"He will not fall. He never does."

Fantine knew she wouldn't win the argument, even if she brought up that Mr. Tugs shuffled along at a snail's pace wherever he went. By the time the man got the ladder from the carriage house to the office, supper would be over. She might as well fetch it herself. "I will see what I can do."

"*You* will see what Mrs. Fraser is up to in the kitchen," Mrs. Pettigrew countered. "I will have Mr. Tugs see to the ladder."

Fantine nodded, suppressing a groan as she left to do her employer's bidding. At this rate, she'd never find out what happened to Mr. Comfort and his brothers in Clear Creek. And why would there be letters by so many different people? Shouldn't there only be two at most, from the mail-order bride and her groom? As she hurried downstairs to the kitchen, she supposed she'd just have to wait to find out. Hopefully, she wouldn't have to wait too long…

Chapter One

Denver, Colorado, October 1877

"If it worked for Pleasant's young man, then confound it, why shouldn't it work for Major?"

Phidelia Hamilton knowingly eyed her brother-in-law, Buford Comfort. "Calm yourself—you'll upset everyone's lunch." They were in one of the nicer cafés in Denver. Several folks looked in their direction, one man in particular, as she took a sip of her tea and set the cup down. "Can't your son find a bride on his own?"

Buford's face turned red. "Didn't you read Pleasant's letters? That backwards town is devoid of eligible women! How can the family line carry on if that boy doesn't take a wife? I've got to think about the future of my dynasty!"

She arched an eyebrow and tried to ignore the onlookers. "You have five other sons, Buford. One of them can see to it."

"Only if he has a wife! Besides, Major is the oldest. It's his duty to go first!"

"You make it sound as if he's to walk the plank. Besides, don't you think Major is capable of seeing to this himself?"

"Major? Heavens, no!"

Phidelia rolled her eyes. Ever since Buford lost his plantation, Comfort Fields, and came to live with her in Denver, he'd been a burden to live with. He'd tried to force his daughter to wed Rupert Jerney—a carpetbagging Yankee cad of the worst sort, but a carpetbagging Yankee cad willing to bail Buford out of a desperate financial situation in exchange for his daughter. Pleasant, the daughter, had not only refused the deal but fled to the other end of the country, finally landing in Oregon as a mail-order bride.

So Comfort Fields was lost…except in Buford's mind. He talked as if the plantation was still in its glory days. If one didn't know the real circumstances, one would think he was still a wealthy man. Instead, he was penniless, surviving on the largesse of his late wife's sister, guilt-ridden over how he'd treated his only daughter—and inclined to bombastic outbursts in public places.

But, Phidelia mused, he was family, and thus her cross to bear. "I suppose I could contact Mrs. Pettigrew."

"Pettigrew?"

"Yes, the matchmaker. She helped Pleasant find a husband well enough and comes highly recommended. She is, however, er…"

"What?"

Phidelia grimaced. "Odd."

"I don't care if she stands on her head and sings 'Old Dan Tucker' as long as she can get the job done!"

Phidelia nodded. "Very well, then. We'll see her tomorrow. Now let's finish our lunch in peace, shall we?"

"Oh, very well." He stabbed at the chicken and dumplings on his plate. "I miss my cook! I can't wait to get back to Georgia!"

Phidelia sighed and tried to hide her concern. There was no cook waiting for Buford back in Georgia—or much of anything else except creditors. He was going mad at a rapid pace. Best she humor him for now and let him believe that his dear Comfort Fields was still alive and well, until he either reconciled himself to the truth or slipped the bonds of sanity altogether.

Clear Creek, Oregon, a month later...

Honoria Alexandra Cooke was the name her parents had bestowed upon her, thinking it grand indeed. To Honoria, it was simply a mouthful. But she wondered what it would be like if it were, say… Honoria Alexandra *Comfort*? Hmmm…she might have to think about that.

Major Quincy Comfort—"Major" was his Christian name, not a rank—was certainly a worthy prospect. He had a deep, smooth Southern drawl, lush dark hair, ice-blue eyes. He was of good antebellum stock—hadn't his family owned a plantation before the War? And tall, too—she guessed the top of her head would just reach his nose. But she couldn't be certain about that, having never gotten to stand close enough to him to check.

Before Major Comfort and his five brothers descended upon Clear Creek last spring, she'd begun to despair of finding a husband anytime soon. But now she had six to choose from! Of course, after hearing a few conversations between her father and her Uncle Colin, only two or three were considered old enough to be husband material. The rest, in their opinions, were still too immature and unsettled. Unsettled, indeed—how could they not be? After all, their family fortune had been lost, and they'd crossed the continent to Clear Creek to retrieve their sister Pleasant, now married to Eli Turner.

If not for a jailbreak in the middle of Pleasant and Eli's wedding, Honoria wouldn't have taken as much notice of the eldest Mr. Comfort as she had. As it was, she got as close as a single young lady was allowed in Clear Creek when Doc Waller asked her to help him patch the man up. Eli, Eli's brother Tom the sheriff, and a posse that included the Comfort men had managed to round the miscreants up after their escape, but not without injuries. Major took a bullet from an outlaw that had managed to sneak up behind him, and suffered a broken rib or two besides.

That had been late spring, though, and now it was an unseasonably warm mid-November, well past harvest time. Major should be long since healed up. But she hadn't seen hide nor hair of him or his brothers for months.

She lay back in the soft grass, plucked a few blades and watched leaves drift down from the giant oak. The tree had been dubbed "His Majesty" decades ago by her grandmother Honoria, for whom she'd been named. It was massive, impressive to look at, and for some reason gave her a feeling of peace whenever she sat beneath it.

She stared up at snippets of blue sky through the canopy of leaves. Soon the mighty tree would lose all its foliage, which she and her siblings and cousins would gather into huge piles, burying each other a few times before burning them. It was one of her favorite events of autumn, a Cooke family tradition, and she looked forward to it every year.

She sat up, leaned back on the palms of her hands and stared at the creek for which the town was named. It flowed into a deep pool beneath His Majesty's branches, and she contemplated whether or not to go wading into it. Finally she decided against it. With her luck she'd slip, fall in and get drenched. She certainly didn't want to ride into town soaked to the skin.

With a sigh Honoria got up, brushed bits of dirt and grass off her skirt and walked to where her horse Rowley stood munching on the meadow grass. Before she mounted, she looked at the spot her father and uncle had cleared for a cabin they never got around to building. It was supposed to be for her Uncle Duncan and Aunt Cozette to use when they returned to Clear Creek to visit, but as the Duke and Duchess of Stantham, their duties in Sussex and London kept them so busy they hadn't been able to come since she was twelve.

Good heavens, that was six years ago! They were definitely overdue for a visit…or if she were lucky, she'd get to visit them. She'd overheard her parents talking of it a few months ago, but hadn't heard anything since. The grate in the floor of her room allowed her to listen to everything going on in the kitchen, which was where most of the family conversations took place. She usually knew what was going on in the family long before anyone told her.

Honoria chuckled at the thought, mounted her horse and adjusted her skirt. She was using her grandmother's sidesaddle, and was proud she could use it to ride as well as any man. She'd like to see Major Comfort try that! Of course, if things kept going the way they were, she'd be lucky to see him or any of his brothers before she reached spinsterhood.

She wasn't sure if it was divine intervention keeping her from the Comfort men, or her father. It was well known in Clear Creek that Harrison Cooke could be zealously overprotective. Take today, for instance—her mother wanted her to go to the mercantile to pick up a few things, but her father insisted she go in midmorning…when the men in the camp outside of town (including the Comforts) would be busy laboring elsewhere.

Oh well. Mr. Dunnigan at the mercantile was always a good source of gossip. Maybe she'd find out more today about how they were doing. She gave her horse a little kick and trotted across the meadow to the trail that led out of the canyon.

By the time she reached town, she wished she'd gone wading. It was already hot and growing hotter, feeling more like July than November. Maybe Mrs. Dunnigan would have some lemonade on hand. She tethered her horse to a hitching post alongside several others, grabbed an empty satchel she'd brought to carry her purchases, wiped her brow and entered the mercantile. "Hello, Mr. Dunnigan. Did Willie bring the mail yet?"

"Howdy, Miss Honoria." Wilfred Dunnigan smiled and winked. "He sure did. Including a letter from your Uncle Duncan."

"Uncle Duncan! How wonderful! That will make the family happy."

"Makes me happy," he said. "Been a while since he's written."

"Yes, I know," she said. "I hope I'll get to visit him soon."

"You mean, go to England?"

"Don't sound so surprised, Mr. Dunnigan. I *am* old enough to travel."

"Not by yourself, young lady. Your pa'd bust a gut before he let you travel alone and you know it. I can hear him groaning now."

Honoria placed the satchel on the counter. "I can dream, can't I?"

"No law against dreaming. You gotta list for me?"

She pulled the list out of her skirt pocket and placed it on top of the satchel. "Mother just needs a few things."

Wilfred nodded, pulled some mail from the stack at the end of the counter, handed it to her and picked up the list. "I'll take care of this right away. Irene made some lemonade, on account it's so warm today. Why don't you go upstairs and say hello?"

Honoria smiled. "You read my mind. I could use a glass."

"Should be getting cooler soon. Them trees are losing more leaves every day." He looked at her list. "Pretty soon they'll all come down, then next thing you know it'll be Thanksgiving."

Honoria sighed. "And after that, another year gone."

Wilfred looked up from the list. "You anxious to get it over with?"

"No, it's just… I don't know, Mr. Dunnigan. It's been so quiet around here since Eli and Pleasant married."

"Yeah," he agreed. "And I hope it stays that way. Last thing I want is another passel of outlaws coming through here stirring up trouble. That last batch did enough damage."

"True enough. Speaking of which, have you seen any of the wounded?"

Wilfred chuckled. "If'n you're referring to Mr. Comfort…" He paused and leaned to peer past her at the mercantile doors. "…why don't you ask him yourself?"

"What?" Then she heard the bell above the door ring. She turned…and in walked the man himself! Her stomach did a flip.

Mr. Comfort stopped short when he saw her, his eyes locking on hers. "Miss Cooke."

She stared back. His clothes were dirty with bits of sawdust, as if he'd been chopping wood or cutting down a tree. His jaw was covered with a couple days' growth of whiskers, and her heart fluttered at the sight. He looked rugged and handsome—so much so that she had to look away.

She listened as the heels of his boots clomped across the wood floor to the counter and stopped next to her. "Is something wrong, Miss Cooke?"

Honoria looked up at the sound of his soothing voice,

and met those wonderful piercing blue eyes. His hair was much longer than the last time she'd seen him—logical, as Clear Creek didn't have a barbershop. Mr. Mulligan would give those residing at the men's camp a snip gratis, as men in those circumstances needed to save money or spend it on food rather than haircuts and shaves. She had no objections—he looked divine.

"Do you see something you like, Miss Cooke?" he asked, startling her out of her observations.

She straightened. "N-nothing."

He took a step toward her. "Are you sure?"

His questions took her by surprise. She fought the urge to gulp and instead gave him a bold stare. "Why? Should I be seeing something?" She made a show of examining him more closely. In truth, she *was* examining him more closely. "Have you something between your teeth, perhaps?"

He chuckled low in his throat. "I certainly hope not, as I'm talking to a lady of refinement."

Drat. He *would* compliment her. She straightened further. "Right, then. Carry on."

She watched him fight a smile into a smirk. "Don't mind if I do." He stepped around her to the counter. "Mr. Dunnigan."

"Mr. Comfort," said Wilfred. "How are all them brothers of yours doing?"

"Working hard, but getting used to it."

Honoria knew she shouldn't, but she did. "Not used to hard work? Is that what being a plantation owner means, that you don't get your hands dirty?"

Wilfred's eyes darted between the two as if he expected a fight to break out. Honoria found hers flicking between Wilfred and Mr. Comfort. For Heaven's sake, it was only a snide remark...

"If you must know, Miss Cooke, the running of a ranch and the running of a plantation are very different," Mr. Comfort explained. "Your family raises cattle. We raised cotton, among other things."

Naturally, Honoria couldn't resist asking the inevitable. "Did you keep slaves?"

"Honoria Cooke!" Wilfred gasped behind the counter. "What kind of a question is that?!" He and his wife were from the South, but had certainly never owned slaves.

"I'm simply curious," she said with a shrug. "Besides, why shouldn't I ask? The war is over, and any slaves are long since freed. I just want to know."

"Yes, we did," Mr. Comfort said stiffly, and turned back to Wilfred. "I've been sent to pick up a few things for the camp. Here's my list." He handed a piece of paper to Wilfred.

"Did you…buy and sell them?" she asked, her voice softer.

"It was my father's job to oversee them, Miss Cooke, not mine. Now if you don't mind, I'd like Mr. Dunnigan to fill my list so I can leave. I'm due back at the camp soon."

Honoria felt a tiny prick of shame. She really had wanted to know, but she realized she'd been rude to ask so blatantly—and in public at that. "I'm sorry… I'm sure you think I'm impertinent."

"You *are* impertinent," he said without looking at her. Wilfred cringed as he reached for a jar on a high shelf.

Honoria cringed with him. "My curiosity always did get the best of me, Mr. Comfort. I *am* sorry."

"You're forgiven, Miss Cooke. Understand, you've lived a different life than my brothers and I, not to mention my sister. But our old way of life is gone and has been for some time. Thanks to this town, we're learning how to leave it behind and live a new one."

She smiled in relief—at his willingness to forgive, at his changing the subject, and at the truth of his statement. The people of Clear Creek were generous, always willing to help. "Have you found much work over the last few months?"

"Yes, here and there. We've even helped your father and uncle a few times."

"You have?" she said innocently. Of course she knew that, but she'd never seen them at the ranch.

"Oh yes. Last month we helped with some of the branding."

"What about now? Are you keeping busy?"

He shrugged. "Some of us. Darcy has made fast friends with the Brodys, and helps in the hotel when he can. Zachary and Michael helped Mr. Mulligan fix things in the saloon over the last couple of months, and plan to help him repaint the front before the weather turns. Matt and Benedict have been helping a farmer, a Mr. Brown, I believe, but they're at loose ends now that the harvest is past. As am I, which is why I'm running errands. We're thinking of setting up a little side business cutting and selling firewood once the cold sets in."

She smiled nervously. "Thank you for all the information."

He leaned against the counter and studied her a moment. "Well, you do seem the type that wants to know all the details."

Wilfred snorted, caught himself, then got back to work.

Honoria blushed and bit her lower lip. She knew she was lucky Wilfred hadn't dissolved into hysterics. "I admit the truth of that," she finally said. "Though as I've already told you, my curiosity can get the better of me."

"As it would seem," he said.

"Well… I'm glad to hear that you're getting on well."

She walked over to a table laden with ribbons, combs, brushes and other paraphernalia, picked up a green ribbon and pretended to examine it.

"That's a good color for you," he commented.

She glanced at him. "You think so?"

His mouth curved up to one side. She wasn't sure if he was smiling, or smirking again. "I do."

She hadn't expected that. Heavens, was he flirting with her? Then again, hadn't she been doing the same? She set the ribbon down and turned to face him. "But I have enough ribbons for now. I don't need another."

He gazed at her appraisingly. "A woman can never have too many ribbons, in my opinion."

She wasn't sure if she liked this or not. Part of her wanted it; part of her was frightened by it. "Oh, I've enough fripperies at home, thank you."

He went to the display table, picked up the ribbon and rubbed it between his fingers. "Silky," he said in a low voice. "Such a thing should adorn hair that feels the same." He purposely gazed into her eyes.

Her face went crimson. How embarrassing! Even Mr. Dunnigan, that hopeless romantic, was staring, waiting for her to respond. But she was stunned into silence. Wishing a man you liked would pay attention to you was one thing—having him actually do it was another! And worse, she could see by his smirk that he knew the effect he was having on her. Drat the man!

"I take it that's your horse outside?"

"What?" she said. Oh—he'd changed the subject again. Rather chivalrous of him, really—he knew he'd embarrassed her and was giving her an out. She took it. "There were several outside when I got here, Mr. Comfort. To which are you referring?" Her voice sounded too terse even to her.

"The one with the sidesaddle. I didn't think anyone around here rode in such a fashion."

"There are a lot of things about Clear Creek, Mr. Comfort, that might surprise you." No, no—that came out all wrong!

But he only smiled again. "Of that, Miss Cooke, I have no doubt."

She swallowed hard. He was still doing it, making her as wobbly as a newborn foal.

The bell above the door rang, drawing everyone's attention. A woman entered, wearing a brown traveling suit with white velvet trim and a hat to match. Honoria's mouth watered at the sight—she'd never owned anything so beautiful—and unconsciously fingered her simple blue calico. For a moment she considered ducking behind the curtain that led to the back to run upstairs and get some lemonade, but her curiosity held her fast.

As Honoria studied the newcomer, she almost winced. Besides being dressed in the latest fashion, the woman was pretty, with blonde hair and dark eyes fringed with long lashes. She sashayed to the counter, a parasol tucked under her arm and a pretty smile in place. "I beg your pardon," she said in a Southern drawl, but one different from the Comforts or the Dunnigans, "perhaps you could help me? I'm new in town, and the person I was to meet hasn't arrived yet."

"Oh, ah…well," Wilfred stammered as he gaped at her. "New in town, eh? Are you here visiting relations?"

The woman looked shyly at the floor. "No, I don't know anyone here as yet."

Honoria shook herself out of her envy. The least she could do was put her nosiness to good use and help the stranger. "Who was supposed to meet you?"

"A gentleman. You see…" She smiled at each of them. "…I'm a mail-order bride."

"A mail-order bride!" Wilfred exclaimed excitedly and slapped the counter. "Great jumping horny toads! Did you hear that, Honoria? Just like all your British aunties!"

Honoria nodded at him, then turned back to the woman. "If you don't mind my asking, who is your intended?"

The woman paused before speaking, looking at each of them in turn. "His name is…well, it's rather odd, I suppose, but it's Major Comfort."

Chapter Two

Major froze. Had he heard the woman right? Judging from the stunned look on Wilfred's face and the horrified one on Miss Cooke's, he had. "And you are?"

"Oh," she said with a silly giggle. "Forgive me for not introducing myself first. I'm Miss Lucretia Lynch. I've come to get married."

Major slowly nodded. "You said that."

The woman flicked a hand at him. "Oh, so I did. I must be tired from my journey. You don't know where I might happen to find Mr. Comfort, would you?"

Miss Cooke had gathered her wits by now and took on a knowing look. What did she think of him now? Not that he'd cared what she thought of him before, mind, but the girl had a quick wit and who knew what was brewing on the tip of her tongue? He'd better jump in before it was too late…

Too late. "Oh, I'm sure he's around," Miss Cooke said, her eyes narrowing slightly at him. "In fact, there are quite a few Mr. Comforts in town. Are you sure you have the right one?"

"Of course I'm sure," the woman said, seemingly offended. "A name like 'Major Quincy Comfort' is not one I'd soon forget. Besides, it's on the marriage contract."

Major grimaced and coughed. "Marriage…contract?"

Wilfred's mouth fell open as his eyes popped and drifted in Major's direction.

"Maybe he forgot he sent for one," Miss Cooke suggested, folding her arms across her chest and smiling at him. He could tell she was enjoying this.

Clearly he needed to take control of the situation before who-knew-what happened. "I don't think Mr. Comfort could forget something he knew nothing about," he said sternly.

"What's *that* supposed to mean?" Miss Lynch asked, glaring at him.

"Only that someone is either pulling a vicious joke, or…" He stopped short. *Oh no, it couldn't be...no, it most certainly could.* "…or my father got some wild idea in his head. That would make some sense out of this."

Miss Lynch looked ready to "lose her religion," so to speak. "And you are?"

He drew in a deep breath. Nothing for it. "My name, ma'am, is Major Quincy Comfort."

"Oh! Then you're…you're…"

"*Not* your intended, alas," he stated. "I'm afraid there's been some sort of mistake—"

"Mistake?" she yelped before he could finish, her voice jumping an octave. "Outrageous! How could there be a mistake? I have the contract in my trunk!"

He looked around, but she had nothing with her save her reticule. "Where are your belongings, Miss Lynch?"

"Outside with the stage and that witless driver. I told him to take my things to the hotel, but who knows if he's got the brains to."

She was agitated, and for good reason. He supposed if

he was in her position, he'd be upset too. But there was still no need to insult poor Willie. "Well, let's try and get this settled as quickly as possible." A movement caught his eye—Miss Cooke's shoulders slumping in relief. At least someone was able to relax.

"There is *no* mistake, Mr. Comfort," Miss Lynch said haughtily. "I'm your mail-order bride and I intend to get married. I did not travel all this way to turn around and go back."

More's the pity, he thought—her attitude, whether normal or from exhaustion, was wearing on his nerves. "I'm sorry, Miss Lynch, but I was not informed of your coming—or that I was to be married at all."

That caught her up short. "You...you weren't?" she replied, a bit more softly.

"No, I wasn't. The only person I can think of who would do such a thing is my father. He's been acting somewhat... erratically of late, and has hinted often enough in his letters that I should be considering marriage. I am quite sorry you were brought unknowingly into his...scheme."

Miss Lynch went rigid. "Well, I never!" she huffed.

Major was about to continue when someone came stomping down the stairs behind the curtained doorway. It must be Mrs. Dunnigan. *Wonderful*, he thought darkly.

Sure enough... "What's going on down here, Wilfred?" Irene Dunnigan asked as she shoved through the curtains to the storefront. She took one look at the newcomer and narrowed her eyes. "Who are you?"

Miss Lynch gasped. "Is everyone in this town so ill-mannered?"

Irene's eyes narrowed further.

"Now Irene, don't cause yourself a mischief," Wilfred consoled. "This here's Mr. Comfort's mail-order bride."

"Mail-order bride?" Irene barked. She spun on Major.

"You ordered a bride?" Before he could utter a word, her head snapped to Miss Cooke and back. "Whatever for?" Miss Cooke's cheeks flamed brilliant red.

Major gritted his teeth and collected himself. "No, ma'am, I did no such thing."

Mrs. Dunnigan scrunched up her face at him, and he fought the urge to lean back. He'd been in town long enough to know what that look meant. "Well then, what's this woman doing standing right in front of you? If you didn't send for her, who did?"

Major sighed heavily. "That's something I'd very much like to find out." He turned to Miss Lynch. "Could I see this contract, ma'am?"

The woman made a show of straightening her jacket bodice and shifting her parasol under her other arm. "This is most embarrassing I must say. If you'll follow me to the hotel, I'm sure we can get this all straightened out. But know this, Mr. Comfort," she said sternly, her eyes as narrowed as Irene's. "I don't like to be made a fool of!"

"Nor do I." He motioned toward the door. "After you."

The woman turned gracefully on her heel and marched to the mercantile doors with small, precise steps. When she reached them she stood, chin in the air, and waited. Major sighed again, went to the door, opened it and motioned for her to precede him.

She didn't. "And here I thought gentlemen from the South were so much more civilized than this Western riffraff."

"Who're you calling riffraff?" Mrs. Dunnigan barked.

"Calm down, Mrs. Dunnigan, it's all in hand," Major assured. Begrudgingly he offered Miss Lynch his arm. "Shall we?"

"That's more like it," she said with a smile. Together, they left the mercantile.

* * *

It was all Honoria could do not to follow them, but that would certainly be rude. After all, it was really none of her business.

But Mrs. Dunnigan decided to make it hers. "Well, don't just stand there, girl—get after them!"

"What? Me?" Honoria asked, a little shocked.

"Yes, you! I want to know what that woman's about!"

"Why don't you go with her, Irene?" Wilfred suggested. "You know you wanna."

Mrs. Dunnigan scrunched her face up a few times in indecision, then growled. "Very well. Mind the store, Wilfred!" She grabbed Honoria by the arm and headed for the mercantile doors.

"Don't forget my list!" Honoria shouted over her shoulder as she was shoved through.

Mrs. Dunnigan wasn't wasting any time, heading down the boardwalk at a racer's clip. "That woman is up to no good! I know it!"

"But what if it's just as Major… I mean, Mr. Comfort says, that his father is behind it?"

"So what if he is? That woman had an awfully determined look in her eye. I'm telling you she means to stay!"

"And get married?"

"Certainly! Why else would she remain here?"

"What's got you all riled up, Irene?" Honoria looked over to find Grandma Waller, the oldest citizen of Clear Creek, standing in front of the bank, a basket on her arm.

"One of the Comfort men went and got himself in a heap of trouble, that's what!" Mrs. Dunnigan stopped and waited for Grandma to join them.

"I thought I saw the eldest run by. Looked like a woman was with him, but I didn't know who it was."

"Check your eyes!" Mrs. Dunnigan huffed. "She's a

stranger in town—and the kind that likes to sink her claws in a man."

"Now, Irene, don't judge," Grandma chastised. "You don't know that."

"Don't I? I've seen the type. She reminded me of that girl that passed through here with her family some years back—the one that tried brawling in the street with Maddie Van Zuyen!"

Grandma's eyes widened. "Oh, that kind, eh?"

"You mean that Bridger girl Mama and Auntie Belle told me about?" Honoria said to clarify.

"That's the one," Mrs. Dunnigan replied. "And when a woman like that shows up, it's always trouble."

Grandma sobered. "Still, let's not be too hasty in judging the poor thing. If she's here to marry one of the Comforts, shouldn't he deal with her? If'n he sent for her, he must want her."

"That's just it, Grandma," Honoria interjected. "He *didn't* send for her."

"He says his pa did, without telling him," Mrs. Dunnigan added.

Grandma's head swiveled between them. "Land sakes, that puts things into perspective, don't it?"

"Not for Mr. Comfort," Honoria said quietly. After all, what if he slept on it, then decided he wanted to marry her in the morning? Stranger things had happened, especially in Clear Creek. Maybe Miss Lynch was just tired and cranky from the journey, and would turn out to be a real peach after a good night's sleep.

"C'mon, let's go," Mrs. Dunnigan snapped.

"Go where?" Grandma asked.

"To the hotel to see what's happening, of course." She started off again.

"Now hold on, Irene," Grandma called after her. "You're poking your nose in someone else's business."

"I am not!"

"Yes, you are. You have no reason whatsoever to go to that hotel."

Honoria watched Mrs. Dunnigan turn to face Grandma, her face red. Grandma was right, as usual, which made her feel all the more guilty for wanting to come along. "Maybe we should go back to the mercantile, have a glass of lemonade?"

"I will *not* go back to the mercantile! That woman is up to no good!"

Grandma rolled her eyes and shook her head. "Then I'm going with you. Lord knows someone has to keep you from scaring the poor thing to death."

"Scare *her* to death?" Mrs. Dunnigan snapped. "She scares *me*!" She stomped toward the hotel, leaving Honoria and Grandma to stare after her.

"What did she mean by that?" Honoria asked, perplexed.

"Good question, child," Grandma replied. "Let's find out."

By the time they caught up to Mrs. Dunnigan, she was already inside. Lorcan Brody, the hotel manager, raised his head from his seat behind the front counter. "Afternoon, Grandma," he greeted in his Irish brogue.

Grandma stopped short and smiled. "If'n I ever stop using lilac water, Lorcan, you'll never guess it's me."

He grinned. "Lilac water suits you. Never stop using it."

"One of these days I will, just to trip you up! Where'd Irene go?"

"Dining room." He pointed, his sightless eyes trained on them.

Honoria and Grandma headed in that direction. Lorcan's blindness and how he compensated with his other senses was legendary in Clear Creek. He knew almost everyone in town by sound and scent alone. Honoria always marveled at it. The man was a walking, talking miracle.

And speaking of miracles, it sounded like Mr. Comfort would need one... "I will not leave! If you think you can just shove me onto a stage and send me back, then you have another thing coming, Mr. Comfort!"

Honoria and Grandma joined Mrs. Dunnigan near one of the dining tables. Major Comfort sat at another with an irate Miss Lynch as Sally Upton, the hotel cook, laid out a tea service for them, her eyes wide as platters as she listened to the woman's tirade.

"I came all this way to get married and I'm going to do it! Besides, you signed the marriage contract."

Honoria watched as Major (why fight it?) openly gaped. "Ma'am, I did no such thing. Please, let me see that contract."

Sally set the teapot on the table, turned to a cart and picked up a plate of cookies and scones. She was about to set them down as well when Miss Lynch started waving an arm around as if she was going to hit something. Sally's eyes followed the limb, waiting for an opening to set the plate on the table.

"Well, *someone* signed it!" Miss Lynch yelled.

"Probably my father," Major grumbled.

"What seems to be the trouble here?"

Everyone turned to see the newcomer. A distinguished-looking middle-aged man stood at the entrance to the room. He had blond hair and hazel eyes, and his clothes looked to be the latest fashion from Paris: a grey frock coat and matching top hat with light grey trousers and a white waistcoat. Honoria idly wondered how long it would be before his outfit became too soiled to wear. This was

Clear Creek, after all—no cobbled roads or fancy coaches. Dressing as this man did just wasn't practical out here.

"Daddy!"

Honoria's head snapped to Miss Lynch, and saw immediately the resemblance between father and daughter. Well, this was getting very complicated very quickly…

Mrs. Dunnigan, tactful soul that she was, wasted no time. "Who in Sam blazes are you?"

The man turned to the three women. "Archibald Lynch at your service, Madame." Honoria noticed he spoke like an Easterner. Then why did Miss Lynch talk with a Southern accent? She glanced once more between the two. Odd.

Mr. Lynch strolled into the room as if he owned the hotel—even stopping to wipe a white-gloved finger across the back of a chair and inspect it for dust. Everyone else could only stare. Who *were* these people, Honoria wondered.

She wasn't the only one. Major stood and looked Mr. Lynch up and down. "I'll repeat Mrs. Dunnigan's question, sir. Who exactly *are* you?"

"I see no need to repeat my answer."

Major's mouth pressed into a firm line and Honoria wondered if he might be counting to ten. He certainly looked it. Finally he said. "I take it, this is your daughter?"

"Whom else would she be?"

"At this point, I have no idea," Major replied. It was quite apparent, to everyone but the Lynches, that he was becoming agitated.

"As the lady did call me 'Daddy' a moment ago, I thought it obvious."

Major frowned. "Allow me to inquire further, then. What are you doing here? Fathers usually don't accompany their daughters in these instances."

"Can't a father ensure his daughter is marrying the right man? I'll not see her wed to some cowboy miscreant."

"I am not a miscreant, sir."

"Glad to hear it. When's the wedding?"

Major's cheeks flushed. Honoria, realizing this might take a while, pulled out a chair and sat. Mrs. Dunnigan and Grandma followed suit, while Sally pushed the tea cart to their table and started to serve.

"There isn't going to be one, sir," Major stated. "I'm afraid someone else engineered your daughter's coming without my knowledge. I had no part in this."

Mr. Lynch now studied Major carefully, as if he was a new suit he fancied. "Really?"

"Truly. I did not send away for a mail-order bride, sir."

Mr. Lynch held a hand out to his daughter. "Lucretia, where's the contract?"

She leaned over, plucked a satchel off the floor, set it in her lap and began to dig through the contents.

"My daughter has a signed contract, sir, and by Heaven you're going to honor it," Mr. Lynch insisted evenly.

"I did not sign it," Major argued. "Even if I wished to, which I didn't, there is no way I could. I have not visited any such agency, nor have I left the environs of this town in months."

"I was informed you signed it and mailed it to Mrs. Pettigrew," Mr. Lynch countered.

"Mrs. Pettigrew? You mean that strange woman that matched my sister with Eli Turner?"

"I know nothing of that. But we dealt with a Mrs. Pettigrew from Denver, and at no small cost to us."

Grandma grabbed a handful of cookies and started to munch one, her eyes glued to the scene. Mrs. Dunnigan slurped her tea. Sally, settling in for the show, joined them and poured herself a cup. Honoria fidgeted, not sure if she should openly stare like the others, look the other way, or try to sneak off.

"Cost?" Major asked. "Since when does it cost the bride anything? As I recall in my sister's case, the intended groom sends any train or stage fare."

"Exactly!" Miss Lynch said. "Which you failed to do!"

"Because, dear lady, I never sent for a bride."

"Nevertheless," Mr. Lynch continued. "My daughter is here, and she *will* get married."

"I have no objection to that, sir," Major replied. "So long as it is not to me." He turned to leave.

"Why, you disreputable scoundrel!" Mr. Lynch fumed. "That's your name on that contract and I'm going to hold you to it!"

Major walked over to him, bringing them nose-to-nose. "I have yet to see this contract."

Mr. Lynch held his hand out, and his daughter slapped a folded piece of paper into it. With a flick of his wrist, he unfolded it and held it up in front of Major. "Here."

Major backed up two steps and began to read, scowling all the while. Honoria was tempted to move closer and look at it herself.

"You see?" Mr. Lynch said in satisfaction. "Now, are you going to abide by this legal document?"

"This 'legal document' has been falsified," Major replied calmly.

"Do you deny that that's your signature?" Mr. Lynch asked.

"I most certainly do. It's not only a forgery, but a bad one."

"A likely story!" Mr. Lynch quickly folded the paper and stuck it in the inside pocket of his frock coat. "If you don't wish to make arrangements for the wedding, I'll be happy to do so."

Major's mouth flopped open, as did those of the other Clear Creek residents in attendance. Was he joking?

"Thank you, Daddy!" Miss Lynch blurted as she stood. "Can we get a room now? I've had a horrible day!"

"Of course, my dear," he cooed as he offered her his arm. Before anyone could say another word, they made their way out of the dining room and straight to the hotel's front desk.

Chapter Three

Major stood frozen. Part of him wanted to go after them, question them further, but he doubted it would do much good—Mr. Lynch and his daughter wouldn't even face the fact of the forged signature. Great Scott, was the man that desperate to see his daughter married? For that matter, was his own father that desperate to see *him* married?

He sank heavily into his chair and groaned. He'd get it sorted out soon, no doubt, but right now all he wanted was a cup of Mrs. Upton's tea and one of the lemon scones she'd placed on the table. He picked one up, bit into it and let the sweetness take his mind off things.

"Are you all right?"

He looked up. Honoria Cooke stood on the other side of the table, her eyes full of concern. "A little befuddled, but I'll get over it."

"Can I help?"

Before he could answer, Irene Dunnigan and Grandma Waller joined her. "Land sakes, son," Grandma said. "What was all that about?"

"I knew she was up to no good!" Irene huffed.

Major held up both hands to quiet them. "A mistake has been made, ladies, nothing more. I'll settle it after I've had time to think—and speak with my brothers." Perhaps one of them had written to their father, prompting this mess.

"You really didn't know she was coming?" Miss Cooke asked.

He gazed at her a moment before answering. Her social graces might not be the most refined, but she had the warmest brown eyes. Kind, gentle…

"Don't just sit there!" Irene barked. "Answer the girl!"

Major pinched the bridge of his nose. "No, Miss Cooke, I hadn't an inkling. But no need to fret—I'll deal with the situation."

Miss Cooke continued to stare at him with those lovely doe eyes of hers. It was all he could do not to stare right back, get lost in them for a while. "I'm sorry you're having to deal with such nonsense. But I know you'll set things right. I just hope that poor girl wasn't too disappointed."

Major looked past the trio to the lobby. There was no sign of Mr. Lynch or his daughter. Lorcan must've given them room keys and sent them upstairs. "She seems determined to stay in town and marry. I'm sure she can find someone willing." Whoever the poor chap turned out to be.

"Well, if that's what she came to Clear Creek for, there's no shame in it," said Grandma. "Lord knows we have enough single men in town what with you and your brothers, not to mention everyone else at the men's camp."

"True enough," Major agreed. "But how many of them can support a bride?"

"That's a fair point," she conceded. "But if'n you don't fancy her, I'm sure someone else will find a way." She looked at her companions. "Show's over, you two. Ain't you got things to do?"

"Oh yes, I'd best see to my list." Miss Cooke said. "Wilfred should've filled it by now." She gave Major a parting smile, then headed for the lobby.

Grandma eyed Irene. "Well? Satisfied?"

Irene scrutinized him a moment, glanced at the lobby in time to see Miss Cooke go through the hotel doors, then turned her gaze on him again. "I'll be watching," she said, eyes narrowed. "You can count on it."

Major pressed his mouth into a firm line to keep from laughing. "In this instance, dear woman, I'd like nothing more."

Her eyebrows shot up at that. "I'll get to it, then," she said, then turned and left the dining room as well. He'd half-expected her to salute.

Grandma Waller shook her head. "Don't mind Irene. She might be grouchy, but she means well. Though I have to admit, your so-called mail-order bride must've rubbed her the wrong way somehow."

"I know, Grandma—Mrs. Dunnigan is just being protective. And I think Miss Lynch rubbed *everyone* the wrong way today."

"Ain't that the truth? I hope she's just tired—she'll never get anywhere in the world if she's a harpy like that all the time." Grandma shook her head again. "One thing about Irene, though—she is good about keeping secrets. Fanny Fig, on the other hand…"

"Oh yes, dear Mrs. Fig. My sister informed me that if you want everyone in town to know something, just tell Fanny." He stood again. "Now if you'll excuse me, I need to return to the mercantile and get the things I came to town for."

"Well, one thing's for sure, Mr. Comfort," Grandma said. "You're gonna have quite a tale to tell when you get back to the men's camp."

"That I will." He only wished it were about someone else.

Honoria stood and listened as Mrs. Dunnigan told her husband everything that had transpired at the hotel between Major and his so-called mail-order bride. Wilfred stood and listened as he continued to fill Honoria's order. "You don't say?" he'd mutter now and then as his wife prattled on.

But what came out of Irene Dunnigan's mouth was hardly prattle. Honoria could tell the woman was genuinely concerned. Why, she had no idea, but she was acting more like a protective bulldog than a gossip, and was obviously recruiting Wilfred into joining her attempt at keeping the town safe. What sort of harm she thought Mr. Lynch and his daughter could do, Honoria had no idea. But the woman definitely saw danger in the pair.

"...And that's why that woman and her father are *not* allowed in this store!" She finished by smacking her ladle on the counter. Honoria hadn't even seen her grab hold of it. It must've been on a shelf underneath the countertop.

"Calm down, Irene," Wilfred urged. "You act as if you expect them two to rob the bank."

"Wouldn't be the first time someone's tried."

"Maybe they're just as they appear," Honoria suggested. "If they're from back East, or even Colorado where Mrs. Pettigrew is, they've had a very long journey. Miss Lynch is entitled to be a little cranky after making such a trip."

"That's all well and good, young lady—I can understand that," Mrs. Dunnigan replied, a little calmer now. "But what's that *man* doing here with her?"

"He *is* her father," Honoria said, though she wondered the same thing.

"I don't know," Mrs. Dunnigan shook her head. "Seems fishy to me."

"Best drop this whole business, Irene," Wilfred said. "Let Major take care of it. It's *his* business, not yours."

"Well, I've made it mine, and I'm not going to stand by

and see that pair…" She stopped, her face reddening. Good heavens, the woman looked ready to burst!

"Please stop worrying, Mrs. Dunnigan," Honoria said. "Don't let it rile you this way."

The older woman looked at her and snorted. "Mark my words, young lady—that woman and her father are trouble." She disappeared behind the curtain and tromped up the stairs.

Wilfred scratched his head and sighed. "I haven't seen her this worked up since that jailbreak a few months back."

"I'm sure she'll be all right," Honoria replied, more out of hope than conviction.

"I dunno. Irene and me, we're not as young as we used to be. Though she's still a lot better than she was. Years ago, when your Aunt Belle first came to live with us, Irene was a force to be reckoned with. Most folks in town were terrified of her—but not your pa and not your Uncle Colin. I have to admit, she almost drove me to drink back then."

Honoria glanced at the floor. "Uncle Colin and Auntie Belle told me stories. They said it was because of what happened to her father."

Wilfred nodded. "Yeah, that's about right. He was a drinking man, a gambler, liked to chase women. He drove Irene's poor ma plumb loco." He straightened and arranged her purchases on the counter. "But enough of that. I'll wrap these up and get you on your way. This everything?"

"It looks like it, thank you. Except for maybe some lemon drops for the road."

Wilfred smiled. "Coming right up." He turned to grab the candy jar.

The bell above the door jingled, and Major walked in. The sight of him sent Honoria's heart skipping all over. "Hello again, Miss Cooke, Wilfred."

"Got your order stacked at the other end of the counter, Major," Wilfred told him.

He strode across the mercantile floor with purpose. The poor man probably just wanted to get back to the men's camp and forget about Miss Lynch and her father for the time being. Honoria didn't blame him. She watched him reach into his pocket. "How much do I owe you, Wilfred?"

Wilfred glanced at Major's list on the counter. "That'll be six dollars, forty cents." Major counted out the money. Wilfred took it, then turned to Honoria. "Yours is three dollars even."

"Oh yes," she said, just realizing she'd been staring at Major. She pulled the money out of her reticule and handed it to him.

Wilfred gave them an odd-looking smile, took the money and placed it under the counter. "Ever seen Honoria here ride sidesaddle, Major?"

"No," he said as his eyes made their way to hers. "I've not had the pleasure."

"She's mighty good at it," Wilfred said. "Maybe ya ought to escort the lady home."

"Wilfred!" Honoria said as if scandalized. She wasn't, but...well, what would her father think if he saw her coming over the rise with Major Comfort at her side? And what did *she* think? She could start thinking a lot if she let herself...

"I'm just saying," Wilfred began again. "After all, there's new folks in town. Who knows who or what is wandering 'round between here and the Triple-C?" His eyes began to dart between the two, and Honoria could tell he was trying to hide a smile. Good grief, could the man be more obvious? Not that she minded.

"You have a point, sir. Perhaps I'd best escort the young

lady home." Major leaned against the counter. "Besides, it would be nice to see a lady ride as a lady should."

Honoria blushed, but raised an eyebrow. "Even if she challenged you to a race?"

He straightened. "A race? I'd not put a lady in danger by accepting such a foolish challenge."

For some reason, his response irked her. Probably because she wasn't joking—she loved to race and was quite good at it, even sidesaddle. "Well, if you're not up to it…"

"It's not a matter of being up to it, Miss Cooke. As I said, I won't do anything to put you in danger."

She switched tactics. "So you think *I'm* not up to it?"

His eyes flicked to Wilfred and back. *Good luck with that*, she thought. The older man had a happy smile on his face, watching them banter. She placed her purchases in her satchel and smiled.

"I assure you," Major finally replied, "I am well up to the task. But if I am to escort you home, I'd like to get you there in one piece."

"Really?" She turned to Wilfred. "Thank you, Mr. Dunnigan." She slung her satchel over her shoulder and headed for the door. As soon as she reached the street, she untethered Rowley and mounted. When she saw Major come outside, she kicked her horse into a trot and headed down the street.

"Wait, you fool woman!"

Honoria smiled, then kicked her horse into a fast gallop.

"Oh Daddy!" Lucretia whined as she buried her face in his chest. Once in her hotel room, she'd put her belongings in the bedroom, returned to the small parlor and practically collapsed against him.

"There, there, my dear. We'll get this straightened out."

"He doesn't want me! He has no interest in me whatsoever! I feel so insulted, so cheated!"

"Nonsense. The poor man hasn't had time to get used to the idea. Don't worry, he'll come around. There's not a woman like you in this backwoods town. What reason would he have to not want you?"

"That cow-eyed farmer's daughter in the blue dress, for one. She…wasn't completely ugly."

"Oh, but she's probably poor as a church mouse—like the rest of the people in this town. She's nowhere near the lady you are."

That seemed to perk her up. She straightened and stepped out of his arms. "I'm sorry, Daddy, I'm just tired. To show up and find out the man didn't even know I was coming!" She sighed. "What am I going to do?"

"What we Lynches have always done, my dear—soldier on." Archibald checked his pocket watch. "Let's not talk of it anymore. Why don't you rest before supper? That Mr. Brody downstairs tells me Mrs. Upton is an exceptional cook. I don't know about you, but I'm looking forward to a fine meal."

She sat in a nearby chair. "That's because neither of us has had a decent one for days."

"Yes…too bad tea was cut short." He went to the chair's mate, sat and crossed his legs. He began to drum his fingers on his knee.

"What's the matter?" she asked.

"Nothing, my dear. Just thinking."

"While you're at it, why not think about writing Mrs. Pettigrew and finding out what happened?"

"All in good time, my dear, all in good time. Don't worry, I'll see to it in the morning."

"Good. Maybe I'll throw in a few lines and give that woman a piece of my mind. The nerve!"

"Now, now—the gentleman is not at fault, not if his story about the forged signature is true. From the sounds of it, his father is behind this. Why else would he not know you were coming?"

"Why else? Because Mrs. Pettigrew is inept, that's why!"

"I said I would take care of everything. Now be a good girl and get some rest."

Lucretia leaned back in her chair in a most unladylike manner. "I suppose I shall. You know you didn't have to accompany me all the way out here just to see me wed."

"I know. But I wanted to make sure everything went smoothly. Heaven forbid my only little girl should marry some cad."

"Mr. Comfort doesn't seem like a cad. In fact, given the circumstances I think he handled it rather well—like a Southern gentleman. Though he did border on rudeness a few times."

"As did you," her father pointed out.

She shrugged. "I had good reason."

"As did he. Now, leave it. Tomorrow is another day and love will conquer."

"Love? I don't see what love has to do with it. Love isn't something a mail-order bride gets to look forward to at first. I would imagine some never find it at all."

"You'll find it in time," he assured her.

Lucretia sighed. She was tired and angry, and the few sips of tea she'd had earlier did nothing to calm her nerves. "I have to get married, Daddy, I just have to!"

"I know, my sweet. Now do as I say and go lie down."

"Oh, very well, if you insist..."

"I do. I'll call on you an hour before supper."

She rose from her chair. "What are you going to do?"

He stood and reached for his hat. "I think I'll have myself a look at the town, see what sort of place my little girl is going to be living. Who knows, I might decide to stay around."

She made a face. "It's so small. I don't see what would spark your interest."

"My daughter living here," he said solemnly.

She closed her eyes and sighed heavily. "I'm sorry, Daddy. I wasn't thinking."

"You're tired. Please, go rest."

Lucretia nodded and, without another word, went into the bedroom, closing the door behind her.

Archibald Lynch blew out a long breath. There'd been a slight hitch in his plan, but he knew things would work out in the end. They always did.

Chapter Four

Major couldn't believe it—was the girl really that reckless? He hadn't even approached his horse before she'd taken off at a wild gallop! He'd never seen a woman ride sidesaddle at that speed, and the sight unsettled him.

He jumped on his mount and took off after her. Once he caught up to her, he knew he'd be tempted to pull her off her horse and turn her over his knee! But what good would that do? She was a woman, not a child.

He heard her laughter on the wind and urged his horse to go faster. Townsfolk smiled as he sped through town. None of them wore the horrified and disapproving expressions he expected and he began to wonder if this was normal for Miss Cooke. He'd find out when he caught her—or perhaps, *if* he did. The woman's steed was incredibly fast. If anything, he'd catch her just to find out about her mount.

She slowed about a half-mile out of town, and Major wondered if she was letting him catch up. Sure enough, as soon as he came alongside she laughed merrily. "I see nothing funny about this," he grumbled, but it was a lie—part of him wanted to laugh with her. The wind had loosed her hair from its pins, and the long sable locks flowed down her back and spilled over her shoulders. Her dark eyes looked bigger than usual, and he noticed how dark her lashes were against her creamy cheeks…

"Are you ready to race now?" she asked in delight.

"Race? What do you call chasing you through town and across the prairie?"

She playfully shrugged. "Chasing me through town and across the prairie. Or, if you prefer, a warm-up."

He opened his mouth to speak, but sighed instead. "Call it what you like, Miss Cooke, but the idea of a race is nonsense. Do your kin know you ride like this?"

"Who do you think taught me?"

"Certainly not your mother."

"She helped."

He hadn't bantered with her like this since he got shot six months ago, and he liked it. "Your father allows you to race across the prairie sidesaddle at a fast gallop?"

"No—at a fast run," she corrected, challenge in her voice.

Their horses walked side-by-side, occasionally nipping at each other. "I don't think my horse wants to race yours," said Major. "He agrees that a lady should remain a lady."

She brought her horse to a stop. "I am a lady—a lady of the prairie. Not one of your cosseted plantation debutantes, but a lady nonetheless."

That annoyed him—mostly because he knew some of the "cosseted plantation debutantes" she spoke of, and she was right on the mark. They always bored him to tears—one reason he was yet unwed. "And what, pray tell, does a 'lady of the prairie' do when she races like a mad woman?"

Miss Cooke laughed. "She wins, of course!" She gave a low whistle, causing her horse to prance around.

His own mount began to do the same. "Here now, what do you think you're doing?"

"Getting ready. Are you?"

"Confound it, woman, will you get the notion of racing out of your head?"

"No, I won't. Besides, the horses want to."

"I don't care what the horses want!"

"What's the matter, Mr. Comfort? Are you afraid you'll lose…" She leaned slightly toward him. "…to a girl?" And she took off like a shot. Against his will, so did his horse.

He wanted to throttle her—once he caught her, that is. For now, he had to be content with keeping his seat. "Miss Cooke!" he shouted.

She only laughed and urged her horse on.

Thank Heaven that stretch of road was smooth, not riddled with rocks or wagon ruts. The last thing he needed was for one of their horses to go down—especially hers. Her father Harrison Cooke would shoot him when he found out what she'd been up to. He wondered how long it would take his brothers to discover he'd gone missing. "Miss Cooke!" he yelled again.

He'd almost caught up to her when he realized he didn't know where they were racing *to*—she'd never told him where the finish line was. But then she suddenly pointed to a copse of junipers up ahead. "Catch me if you can, Mr. Comfort!" she yelled over the wind. A difficult task at best—it was becoming more and more obvious she had the better horse, but it didn't mean he wasn't going to try.

He gave a sharp whistle. His horse did its best and sped up, giving his master what energy he had left. Soon they were neck and neck, and Miss Cooke's startled yelp at seeing him so close sent a thrill up his spine. She hadn't expected him to catch her. Good—he planned to get a lot closer once they stopped.

And stop they did, almost on top of each other, when a fox darted out from under the junipers and spooked both mounts. The animals skidded to a stop in a cloud of swirling dust and a startled cry. He heard a dull thud and a muffled oath. Great Scott, she must have fallen from the saddle! Worse, he couldn't see her with all the dust in the air—and in his eyes. "Miss Cooke!" he called. "Are you hurt?" He quickly dismounted and scanned the ground.

She lay in a heap, her skirt and petticoats tangled around her thighs and waist. The result was a good amount of exposed—and lovely—calf and knee to him. Major swallowed hard and looked away, gathered his wits and went to her. He still didn't know if she was hurt or not. "Miss Cooke." He knelt at her side.

She looked at him, coughed and grabbed her at her ribs.

"I rest my case. Ladies should not race across the prairie the way *you* just did."

She did her best to snarl at him, but sounded more like a frightened mouse.

Concern filled him and he leaned toward her. "Can you talk?" Poor thing probably had the wind knocked out of her.

She opened her mouth but nothing came out.

"It's all right, stay where you are. Are you in pain?"

She nodded. "I'll be...fine," she whimpered.

"In a pig's eye," he said. "Now lie still until you get your breath back and tell me where it hurts."

She swallowed hard, her eyes pleading, and motioned him closer.

Good heavens, was it that hard for her to talk?! "What is it? What's hurt? Anything broken?" He'd have to check for the latter. But it would be nice to have a place to start.

She pointed at herself. "Only my pride," she said weakly.

Major leaned back on his heels and put his hands on his thighs. "Your pride? That's the only thing that hurts?"

She coughed and spit out some dirt. It was then he noticed how much was on her face. Just how *did* she land? "I'm fine…or I will be. And I won."

"We can debate that later. I'm not sure you're fit to get up yet. Perhaps you can ask the fox who won?"

A small laugh escaped her and she grabbed at her side.

"Are you sure you're not hurt? You might've broken a rib."

She shook her head. "No. I've fallen off enough to know what that feels like. I just need to rest a moment before I get back on my horse."

Major sat. "You're a fool, you know."

"I am not. But I didn't expect that silly fox to come running out. If he hadn't spooked our horses, I would've come in first."

"We'll never know, now will we?" he taunted.

"Then we'll have to have a rematch."

"A rematch! Don't be absurd. Look at you! You can't even sit up yet."

"If you'd taken a tumble, you'd still be on the ground."

He shook his head and rolled his eyes. "But I didn't, did I?" He jumped to his feet, brushing dust from his clothes as he did.

"Where are you going?" she asked.

"To get you some water." He went to his horse, removed the canteen from the saddle horn and returned. He again knelt and helped her to sit up, keeping an arm behind her back for support as he handed her the canteen. "Here, drink some of this. At least get the dirt out of your mouth."

She smiled and did as he asked, took a sip, swished it around in her mouth, spit, repeated the action.

"Better?"

"I don't always land on my face, you know."

"You're lucky you didn't break your neck. Now drink."

"Don't boss me," she shot back, though he noted her

voice was still weak. The fall had taken more out of her than she expected, he could tell. Her hands shook as she lifted the canteen to her lips once more and drank.

When she finished he took the canteen, satisfied his own thirst, then handed it back to her. "Take another small sip." She did, then handed it back. He screwed the cap back on and set it on the ground behind him. "Do you think you can stand?"

"Of course I can stand. I didn't break my leg, you know."

He chuckled. "Pride cometh before a fall," he quoted dryly. "Let me help you up." He stood, went behind her and put a hand under each arm, gently lifting her to her feet and making sure she stayed there. A good thing too, as she began to teeter. Major quickly pulled her close. "Easy now, you're not quite there yet."

"I'll be all right."

The remark was almost laughable. "No, I'm afraid you won't." He gave a low whistle. His horse stopped munching the dry prairie grass, raised its head and nickered, then made its way to them. "I'm going to take you home."

"No! I can make it home by myself."

He heard the panic in her voice but also noted it was still weak and strained. Was she having trouble breathing? Maybe he should take her back to town. "Do you need a doctor?"

"No, I do not need a doctor!" she snapped, and her body went tense against his.

"There's no need to get angry, Miss Cooke. I'm simply looking out for your welfare."

"I've been looking out for my own welfare for a long time, Mr. Comfort. I don't need you to."

"Really?" he said, trying to keep the sarcasm out of his voice. "Well then, since you don't need my help..." He set her firmly on her derrière in the dust, stepped away and went to mount his horse.

She stared at him in shock. "What are you doing?"

"Heading home, of course. Seeing as how you don't need my help, I see no reason to stay."

A flicker of panic lit her eyes. "You're just going to leave me here?"

"As you said, you've been looking out for your own welfare for a long time." He hopped into the saddle, gave his horse a little kick and began to trot away, smiling. He doubted she was really as used to taking care of herself as she claimed, and at this point was willing to let her pride get her into the trouble she so avidly sought.

"All right, fine!" she groaned.

He slowed his horse to a walk and turned him around. He didn't like the sound of her voice, as if it was an effort for her to speak louder. If she hadn't broken any ribs, she'd at least bruised some.

She was trying to stand, but clearly couldn't, not unassisted. "Please, I… I can't do this," she said, her voice cracking.

That did it. He cantered back to her.

"Back so soon?" she croaked and swallowed hard.

He could see the pain in her eyes and knew she was more hurt than she let on. But he also knew she wasn't ready to go easy on herself—or him. "I find myself in a bit of a dilemma." He dismounted. "Perhaps you can help me out."

"What dilemma is that?" she said with a grimace.

"Whether to turn you over my knee and give you the spanking you deserve, take you back to town to see Doc Drake, or take you home and let your father have at you."

She gulped at the mention of her father. "Yes—that is a dilemma, isn't it?"

"What do you think?" he asked, hands on hips.

She shrugged, then winced. Definitely bruised ribs. "I haven't the foggiest."

He glanced at the sun to judge the time. "Well, we have only a few more hours of daylight. I vote for the doctor—we're closest to him." He gently pulled her to her feet, scooped her up in his arms and carried her to his horse.

"What are you doing?" she asked in protest.

"Putting you on my horse. I'd thought it would be obvious."

"I'm perfectly capable of getting on a horse by myself."

"Like you're perfectly capable of standing?" He reached the animal and stood beside it. "Put your foot in the stirrup and reach for the saddle horn. I'll help you mount."

"From this position?" she asked, aghast.

"My dear woman, it will be easier from this position than from the ground. I'll help."

She smiled ruefully, rolled her eyes and did as he instructed. With a little pushing on his part, he got her into the saddle. He retrieved her horse and handed her the reins, then mounted up behind her and traded the reins in her hands for the ones belonging to his horse.

"Now what?" she asked as he put an arm around her waist and gently pulled her against him.

Unable to help himself, he leaned down and spoke into her ear. "Now, Miss Cooke, we go back to Clear Creek. I want Doc Drake to take a look at those ribs. You must've landed on a stone. I noticed a few of them around."

She didn't speak for a moment, and he worried something was wrong. "Very well. But my family won't be happy if I don't get home soon."

"I'll speak to them myself when we get there."

"What? We?!"

"It'll be growing dark by the time we leave the doctor's.

I can't allow you to ride home by yourself, especially not in your condition."

"I've done it before."

"Good for you. But not today."

She gasped, and he wanted to put his other arm around her, but didn't dare. "Let's go," he said quietly. He gave his horse a little kick and they were off—in the wrong direction. "For Heaven's sake, woman, you have the reins. Turn this horse toward town."

"Oh. Yes. Sorry."

All the bravado seemed to have gone out of her, and he found he missed it. Maybe she was distracted by the pain. "If you like, I can handle both pairs of reins, or..."

She didn't reply, only turned the horse around.

"It's gratifying to know there's a part of you that sees reason," he said playfully.

Thankfully, she caught his tone rather than taking offense. "And the other parts?"

"I hesitate to think..."

She tried to speak, took a breath and remained silent.

"Are you having trouble breathing, Miss Cooke?" he asked, his voice gentler.

"Yes," she finally said.

He held her closer. "Don't worry, we're not far from town. Doc Drake will fix you right up." She nodded and let her head fall limply against his shoulder. She was obviously in more pain than she was letting on. "I'll see you're well taken care of, Miss Cooke," he promised. "You can count on that."

She took a shuddering breath. "I know," she groaned.

Chapter Five

Honoria tried to keep her breathing under control. For one, it hurt; for another, she didn't want to look like more of an idiot than she already did. But more of an idiot is what she'd become if Major Comfort—who at the moment was living up to his name—held her any closer. Having his strong arm around her was overwhelming, and when that deep Southern drawl caressed her ear, it was all she could do to stay in the saddle! Her heart raced, her breathing quickened (painfully so), and she wanted desperately for him to put his other arm around her.

But as he held Rowley's reins in his free hand, that wasn't going to happen. Too bad it was such a short ride back to Clear Creek. She wouldn't mind being like this for an hour or two longer.

All too soon, they'd reached Doc Drake's. Major slid off the back of his horse, then stepped around his horse and helped her down—or rather, he gently let her slide into his arms. "Are you planning to carry me into Doc Drake's?" she asked, trying to hide her hopefulness.

"Yes, I am." He headed for the porch steps.

"I'm perfectly capable of walking…" No, she wasn't—

and why was she arguing with the man? Hadn't her pride gotten her into this predicament in the first place?

From the look on his face, he knew she wasn't either. "Let's not take any chances, shall we?" He reached the porch, tapped on the door with his boot a few times then waited.

Grandma Waller swung the door open and gasped. "Land sakes, what happened to you?"

"A fox spooked my horse," Honoria answered quickly. Who knew what Major would say?

She soon found out. "Her horse came to a sudden stop because of it. Unfortunately for Miss Cooke, she didn't."

Well, that could've been worse—at least he didn't mention the racing, or embellished with some sarcastic remark. But she was beginning to see he wasn't that kind of man. He'd tease her, yes, but he wasn't cruel.

Grandma shook her head and narrowed her eyes. "Honoria Cooke, how many times has your father told you about racing that horse of yours across the prairie?"

Honoria groaned. So much for worry about Major mentioning it. "Thank you, Grandma."

Major's eyebrows slowly rose in amusement. "I see. Well, I think your father and I will have a very interesting conversation later."

She groaned again. "You wouldn't."

"Of course I would. And I'll enjoy every minute of it."

He was teasing again, she knew. "You're horrid, you know that?"

"I have my moments."

Grandma stepped aside to let them in. "Take her into the back, Mr. Comfort. You know the way."

"After all we've been through, please, call me Major." He carried Honoria over the threshold. An image of being in a wedding dress flashed in her mind's eye, and she shivered. "Are you all right?" he asked, concerned.

"Yes," she said, but her voice betrayed the truth. She needed to get a hold of herself! That was no easier when he set her on the bed in the patient room. A chill went up her spine at the sudden loss of contact, and she caught herself looking longingly at him. She frowned and glanced away. The next thing she knew, she'd be looking at him all moony-eyed! What would Grandma think?

Actually, knowing Grandma, she'd encourage it.

"Bowen's outback with Ellie in the barn, Major," Grandma said. "Best go fetch him. I'll put on some coffee—you both look like you could use some."

"Thank you," Major studied Honoria for a moment, concern in his eyes, then quickly left.

"Well, that's that, then," she whispered to herself. Now she was Doc Drake's problem, no longer Major's. The thought made her feel empty except for all the aches.

"You all right?" Grandma asked from the doorway. "A tumble can do strange things to a body."

"I...well, I'm not fine, but I don't think anything's broken." She paused before adding, "Though it hurts to breathe."

"Foolish child," Grandma scolded. "You're lucky you didn't land on your head!"

"It wasn't my fault, Grandma."

"It never is."

That stung. "What is that supposed to mean?"

"You were showing off for him, weren't you?"

Honoria gulped. "No, I was...well... I...oh, all right, maybe a little."

Grandma put her hands on her hips. "Honoria Cooke, why can't you flirt like other girls? You don't have to pull a death-defying feat to get a man's attention, you know!"

"A race is hardly death-defying, Grandma."

"In this case it almost was." Grandma came back into the room, pulled some bandages from a cupboard and set them on the table by the bed. "Bowen's probably gonna want to wrap those ribs of yours." She pointed at her. "Don't move. I'm gonna go make that coffee." She left.

Honoria was now alone with her thoughts, none of them pretty. She was angry, mostly at herself. Grandma was right—she had been showing off challenging Major to a race. And what did she get for her trouble? Bruised ribs and bruised pride. At the moment, she didn't know which hurt worse. And what a storm this would cause when her overprotective father found out! She just hoped Major wasn't there to witness it—what would he think of her then?

She laid her head against the pillows and groaned. By tomorrow, Miss Lynch would be looking much more a lady in Major Comfort's eyes. And she much more a fool.

"Does this hurt?" Doc Drake asked as he poked and prodded at Miss Cooke's ribs, while Major leaned against a nearby hutch.

"Ouch," she yelped as he got to a particularly tender spot.

The doctor leaned back in his chair and gave her a look that said, *well, you've done it again.*

"Bruised ribs?" she asked sheepishly.

"You're lucky that's all. At least you didn't give yourself a concussion like the last time."

Ah, just as he thought. Major stood up straight. "The last time? So this is not Miss Cooke's first visit here?"

"Hardly," said the doctor, turning to Major. "It's a good thing you were there when it happened."

Major arched a single eyebrow and smiled at Miss Cooke. "Yes, wasn't it though?"

"You've healed nicely," the doctor commented to him.

"Thanks to you and Doc Waller, yes."

Doc Drake offered Major his hand. "Call me Bowen. You and your brothers have been here long enough—you're part of the community."

Major shook his hand. "Call me Major then."

Miss Cooke rolled her eyes. "And one of you can call me a hansom cab to take me home."

The men laughed. "I'm afraid you're not in London, Honoria," Bowen said. "But when your father gets a hold of you, you'll wish you were."

"Funny, Grandma said something similar when she served coffee earlier," Major quipped.

"Will you stop bringing him up?" Honoria groused. "I don't want to think about my father."

"Yes, I suspect we won't be seeing you around town for a while," Bowen commented dryly.

"Why not?" Major asked.

Bowen turned to him again. "Because Harrison will ground her on the ranch—or worse, take away her horse—to teach her a lesson."

"Doc Drake!" she whined. "Please, stop."

"Not that she's likely to learn it, mind you."

"Well, well," Major chuckled. "I'm discovering all sorts of things about you today, Miss Cooke."

She frowned and turned her head to stare at the opposite wall.

"I'm still taking you home, you know," he added for good measure.

She still didn't look at him. "Please don't."

"You leave me no choice. I was there when you fell. I'm responsible."

"The fox is responsible."

"Nevertheless, I brought you to town to have you

tended, so I should be the one to take you home. No arguments."

She sighed and finally turned her head back—to glare at him.

"You don't have to like it," he offered.

"Oh, I don't."

It was all Major could do not to laugh—she was adorable when she was angry! "Any gentleman worth his salt would do the same."

That softened her expression, and her eyes met his. She almost looked guilty—almost. "Very well, then—you may accompany me home."

Bowen, through patching her up, sat back in his chair. "She's all yours, Major. Though I don't know how well she'll be able to sit a horse."

"She'll ride with me," Major said. "That's how I got her here." Something flashed in her eyes but he wasn't sure what it was. Was she still angry? If so, too bad.

"Rather improper, don't you think?" she asked.

"I could hitch up the wagon," Bowen offered. "Take you home myself."

"No," Major said before Miss Cooke could agree. "I'll take the lady home. I'd like to speak to her father."

She stared at him open-mouthed. "But…you have nothing to say to him."

"Oh, don't I? On the contrary, Miss Cooke, I've quite a few things I'd like to say to him. And not just about your reckless riding habits."

Her eyes widened. Good—stewing a while would probably benefit her. If her English father had any idea how unladylike his daughter had acted today, he'd probably… hmmm. What *would* Harrison Cooke do? Major and his brothers had dealt with the Cookes on several occasions since their arrival, and found them good, honest, hard-working men. But how a man behaved in public with a hired laborer and in private with his offspring were often two different things.

"What?" she asked.

"I beg your pardon?"

"You seemed deep in thought. What about?"

"None of your business," he said.

"Well, I'm done with mine," Bowen said as he stood. "She's all yours, Major."

"Thank you, Doctor."

"Bowen," he said with a smile.

"When you're working I'll call you *Doctor* Drake."

"Fine with me—a lot of folks do." He turned to Miss Cooke. "As for you, Honoria, please be more careful from now on."

"I'm going fox-hunting next, just so you know."

Both men laughed. "I pity the fox," Major said, then carefully helped her swing her legs over and place her feet on the floor. He was looking forward to their ride to the Triple-C. It meant having an arm around her again, the scent of her hair in his nostrils, the feel of her soft body against his as they rode…

"You want some cookies to take with you?" Grandma asked as she poked her head in.

Major jumped, startling Miss Cooke. She yelped accordingly.

"Land sakes, what did you do, step on her foot?" Grandma entered, a small bag in her hand.

"No, Grandma," Miss Cooke said, giving Major the side-eye. "He just surprised me, that's all."

"I'm sorry," Grandma said. "My fault for barging in without knocking." She handed the bag to Major. "Here, some molasses cookies for the road."

"Thank you kindly." He took it and handed it to Honoria. "You hold it in case I have to carry you."

"Carry me?" she snapped, then looked down in embarrassment.

Major chuckled. "No offense meant, Miss Cooke. I'm just trying to make sure you're taken care of."

Grandma smiled. "Well now, Mr. Comfort, that's very gentlemanly of you." She glowered in Miss Cooke's direction. "Ain't that right, Honoria?"

Miss Cooke's jaw tightened. "Yes, Grandma."

He smiled. At least Grandma Waller was on his side. "Very well, then—let's be off." He helped Miss Cooke to stand, then, just because he wanted to, swept her into his arms.

She wrapped her own arms around his neck, a mischievous gleam in her eye. *Uh-oh.* "What happened to, *in case* you have to carry me, Mr. Comfort?"

Two could play at this game. "But I thought you *liked* being in my arms, Miss Cooke."

She gasped.

"Faker."

Now she growled!

"Oh, stop acting so perturbed, Honoria," Grandma scolded. "How often do you have a handsome man carry you to your horse?"

"Grandma!" Bowen said as if thoroughly scandalized, but winked at Major. Aha, so the doctor sided with him as well. This was getting better by the minute!

Miss Cooke, sensing she was outgunned, stayed silent until they got outside. Once on the porch, she looked up and groaned.

"Am I holding you too tight?" he asked. All teasing aside, it was a genuine concern.

She turned her head into his shoulder, as if trying to

hide. "No, but we're in for it now. Look over at the mercantile."

Major looked...and saw Fanny Fig standing in front of the mercantile, staring right at them. "Oh dear."

"Exactly. Who knows what she'll say about this."

He shook his head, walked down the steps and headed for the horses. "If—or should I say, *when*—she starts any rumors, I'll take care of it."

Miss Cooke blinked a few times. "You will?"

He stopped and looked at her. "Of course I will," he said, his voice tender. "I'll not see anyone damage your reputation."

She gave him the tiniest hint of a smile. "Thank you."

He smiled back, then began walking again. "Think nothing of it. As I said before, dear lady, these are things any gentleman would do."

She looked away, and he knew he'd embarrassed her. True, she'd been raised by English gentlemen for the most part—but English gentlemen transported to the frontier, far away from high society. He and his brothers had been an integral part of polite company in Savannah until earlier that year. The ruggedness of the prairie and surrounding mountains had yet to beat it out of them. "Let's get you on my horse," he told her. "Do exactly as you did before, and let's see what kind of reaction we get from Mrs. Fig."

She snorted in laughter, then winced. "She might well faint."

"Good—if she does, she won't be able to spread rumors around about us."

"Until she revives. Then she'll probably hurry to make up for lost time."

"Then I'll have to do my best to stand by you, won't I?"

She stared at him in shock.

"What's the matter?"

She shook her head. "N-nothing."

Clearly the woman in his arms was used to doing things on her own, including defending her reputation. Not much of a task when she was younger, perhaps, but now that she was of age... "We'd best be off." He positioned himself next to the horse, just as he'd done before. "Ready?"

"Yes."

He helped her mount, took the reins of her horse and handed them to her, climbed up behind her and positioned himself as before, one arm around her waist, his free hand taking the reins from her so he could lead her horse behind them. "Once again, Miss Cooke, you're in charge. Take us home—and please, no racing."

She sighed and nodded. "As you wish, Mr. Comfort." Her voice had a slight edge to it, but he didn't blame her for that. She was still in pain—and probably smarting over her own headstrong behavior as well. He gave the horse the kick and she directed the animal back the way they came.

Right past Fanny Fig, as it happened. "Honoria Cooke!" Fanny huffed. "What do you think you're doing?!"

"She's injured. I'm escorting her home," Major answered before his riding companion could.

Fanny's mouth opened and closed a few times, looking more than a little flustered. Finally, she managed to shout, "Why, it's indecent! I would think a Cooke would know better!"

"Would you rather she die on the trail trying to make it home by herself, Mrs. Fig?" Major asked calmly but firmly.

"Of course not!" Fanny shot back.

"Then I suggest you thank the Almighty that I'm taking the time to escort her home properly so no more harm comes to her."

"Well...what's her father going to say about this?!"

"Something like, 'thank you, Mr. Comfort,' I should

think," he called over his shoulder as they continued. "After all, that would be the proper response after saving his daughter, don't you agree?"

Once they were out of earshot, Miss Cooke giggled. "Oh my," she said quietly. "What will she do with that?"

"Not much, I suspect. Especially since half the town probably heard our exchange."

"Seems I need to thank you again, Mr. Comfort."

"No need—you've thanked me enough. Now let's get you home."

Chapter Six

By the time Honoria reached the Triple-C, she had come to the startling conclusion that she liked Major Comfort. She'd already known she was attracted to him—he was a very handsome man. But she'd learned over the years that looks weren't everything. She'd heard enough stories from her family and others in town about men, women and weddings, and knew it took a lot more than being attracted to one another to make a relationship work. Though looks did help.

For a time she'd had a crush on Eli Turner, when they were younger. But over the years it became apparent that they would never suit, even if they did like each other. There was always something missing with Eli. Everyone in town thought they'd court, but the truth was that Eli was no more interested in her than she was in him. Once he got a mail-order bride, that was that.

And thank Heaven he'd married Pleasant Comfort, or she wouldn't be in the arms of her brother right now, cresting the rise to get that glorious view of the Triple-C with the setting sun as a backdrop. "Beautiful," Major whispered behind her.

She brought their horse to a stop. "It is, isn't it? I never get tired of this view. I never will."

"Do you plan on living here the rest of your life, then?"

"I could live with that notion."

"To live and die in the same place?"

She turned her head toward his shoulder. "If you hadn't come west after Pleasant, wouldn't you have done the same? Lived and died on your plantation in Georgia?"

He drew in a deep breath and let it out slowly. "No. We were about to lose the plantation already. But I would have liked to."

"Oh, I'm sorry—I didn't realize. Was your plantation large?"

"One of the larger in the area."

"Do you miss it?" It was a touchy subject, no doubt, but she was curious.

"In many ways, yes. Comfort Fields was very special to me, as it was to the rest of my family. It wasn't so much a plantation, Miss Cooke. It was a…a different way of life, even after the war and emancipation. But we learned to cope, work, sweat to survive. It taught me how to be a real man."

She faced forward again. "I'm glad to hear it." And he was every inch a man. He didn't put up with her nonsense—or rather, he didn't take it too seriously and called her on it. She could spar with him, the same as she could with her father and uncle. He was a good match for her…

"Is something wrong?" he asked.

Honoria belatedly realized she'd started at her own realization. Major *was* a good match for her! But did he think so?

"Miss Cooke?"

"Oh yes… I mean, no. Nothing's wrong." She was glad he couldn't see her flushed face.

He gave the horse a kick, and they began their descent toward the barnyard. She scanned their surroundings and saw no one around, which was a relief. She wanted to enjoy his company a few more measly moments before they were interrupted—and to stave off the embarrassment and scoldings to come.

But the respite was short-lived. "What the Sam blazes happened to you?" Grandpa Jefferson barked as he came out onto the front porch of the main ranch house.

She steered the horse to the porch steps and stopped. "I had a little accident, Grandpa," she said sheepishly.

"Again?" Grandpa Jefferson barked. "Oh, for cryin' out loud—yer pa's gonna bust a gut when he finds out!"

"Where is he?" she asked.

"He ain't come back yet—still out workin' the cattle with yer uncle and the rest of boys."

"Thank heavens," she muttered under her breath.

She felt Major lean toward her ear. "Pity," he whispered. "I was rather hoping to chat with him."

His warm breath sent a shiver up her spine and sent her belly into somersaults. "I suppose you'll just have to wait."

He slid off the back of the horse then carefully helped her down. Jefferson noted the way he was handling her and came off the porch to help. "What did ya do this time? You didn't break nothin', did ya?"

The questions did nothing for her mood. "If I had, Grandpa, would I be standing here?"

"Knowin' ya, yeah, prob'ly." He looked at Major. "Tough as nails, this one, but hain't got a brain in her head sometimes."

"Grandpa!"

"What? We all know it. What's wrong with this fella knowin' it too? Not that he couldn't figger it out himself. What'd she do, jump a fence? Run headlong into a tree?"

"Believe it or not, it wasn't Miss Cooke's fault," Major said in her defense. Would wonders never cease?

She gaped at him for a second before she straightened and added, "It was a fox."

"It darted from underneath some juniper trees and spooked the horses," Major further explained. "Miss Cooke was thrown and came to a rather jolting stop. Mine did too, as a matter of fact, but I managed to keep my seat."

"At least one of ya did," said Jefferson. "I'm glad—otherwise ya'd both still be out there. Lord knows she couldn't have hauled *you* back."

Major looked at her and their eyes locked. "Yes, it is a good thing." They both knew it was true. If he'd been the one injured, she'd have had to leave him there and gone to fetch help. And if she couldn't…

"Well, get on inside and let's get this over with," Jefferson said.

"Over with?" Major echoed.

"He means my mother," Honoria said.

"Oh. Is she as…protective as your father?"

"It's a coin toss," Jefferson put in. "Harrison gets louder, but Sadie puts in her fair share."

Honoria sighed and stared at the porch steps. Hopefully it wouldn't hurt too much climbing them, as she'd need all her strength to face Mother. Well, no use stalling. "As Grandpa said, let's get this over with." She let Major and Grandpa help her up the steps and into the house.

Once inside, they discovered the house was relatively quiet, which she took as a good sign. "Yer ma's prob'ly in the kitchen," Jefferson informed her before heading down the hall. Honoria and Major slowly followed.

Sure enough, they found Sadie stirring a pot of something on top of the family's enormous stove. "Great Scott," Major exclaimed. "Look at the size of that!"

"What's the matter, Mr. Comfort?" Honoria said. "Haven't you ever seen a cook stove before?"

"Not one that size."

Sadie turned to the newcomers. "There you are, Honoria—I was wondering when you were going to get home. I need that cinnamon..." She paused to look at Major. "Hello. You look familiar."

"Good afternoon, Mrs. Cooke. Or should I say, good evening?"

"About that." She arched an eyebrow at her daughter. "Where have you been? You should've been home hours ago."

Honoria took a deep breath and grimaced. It still hurt to do that. "I had an accident on the way home."

Sadie stopped stirring and stared at her. "Accident? What kind of accident?"

"A fox jumped out in front of her horse and spooked him," Major explained. "Your daughter unfortunately parted ways with her saddle."

"She fell off?" Sadie looked her daughter over. "You didn't land on your head again, did you?"

"Partly," Honoria said. "This time around my midsection took the brunt of it."

"Doc Drake says she has a few bruised ribs," Major added.

"Bruised ribs!" Sadie put one hand on a hip. "Honoria Alexandra Cooke, just what were you doing?"

Honoria knew she wouldn't get out of this easily. "I suppose it was my fault."

"You suppose?" Major chided.

Sadie closed her eyes a moment and gritted her teeth. "You were racing again, weren't you?"

"Yes, Mama. I was," Honoria said and stared at the floor.

Sadie set down the spoon and put her other hand on the other hip. "And you let her?" she accused Major.

"Me?" he said in surprise. "Allow her? As if I could prevent her. Mrs. Cooke, your daughter took off on her horse as if someone had called for a cavalry charge! I gave chase to try to slow her down."

Honoria fumed. He'd betrayed her as easily as that!

"So you fell for it, eh?" Sadie turned back to the pot on the stove. "When will people ever learn?" She gave the contents another quick stir and set the spoon down again. "Well, Mr. Comfort, since you're here, you might as well stay for supper." She arched an eyebrow at him. "Unless, of course, you feel the need to leave. Immediately."

"You had best take that as a warning," Honoria hissed.

Major glanced between her mother and Jefferson—and called the bluff. "I'd love to stay," he said, a forced smile on his face.

"Good," Sadie said after a moment's surprise. "I'm sure you and Honoria's father will have *all sorts* of things to talk about." She gave Honoria a pointed look. "Won't they, precious?"

Honoria forced her own smile. "I'm sure they will."

Sadie grunted, picked up the spoon and turned back to the pot. "Why don't you take Mr. Comfort into the parlor, Honoria?" She abruptly turned to face them. "Nothing else is hurt?"

"Just the ribs, Mama. I'll be fine."

Her mother visibly relaxed and leaned against the worktable a moment. "Thank the Lord for that." She looked at Major. "And thank you for bringing her home."

Major smiled reassuringly. "It was my pleasure, Mrs. Cooke."

"Well, that wasn't so bad," Major said, taking a seat in one of two matching wing chairs in the parlor.

Honoria glared anew. “We got off easy—and only because she’s waiting for my father. Then we’re in for it.”

“We are hardly schoolchildren, Miss Cooke.”

She was about to comment when Grandpa Jefferson entered, a cup and saucer in his hands. He offered it to Major. “I figgered ya might like a cup of coffee. What kind of hosts would we be if’n we didn’t offer ya somethin’?”

“Thank you, sir.” Major took the cup and saucer from him. “Tell me, do you know when Mr. Cooke will be home?”

“Harrison? Should be back about suppertime.” He smirked and looked at Honoria. “Cain’t wait for tonight’s conversation ’round the table.” With a snicker, he turned and headed for the foyer. “I’ll be in the dinin’ room settin’ the table—holler if’n ya need me.”

“I will, Grandpa,” Honoria said.

“Need him?” Major remarked.

“He’s playing chaperone—setting the table so he can keep an eye on us.”

“Chaperone…oh yes, of course.” Major reminded himself that, frontier or no frontier, he wasn’t dealing with savages. But the irony was palpable—he had ridden with her flush against him, carried her in and out of Doc Drake’s house, ridden close to her again to the Triple-C, and *now* they had a chaperone? He had to chuckle.

“What’s so funny?”

“Oh, nothing.” He took a sip of coffee. “Would you like some? I could go into the kitchen and ask your mother to pour you a cup.”

“No, I never drink coffee before supper. Maybe a cup of tea now and then. Grandpa knows—that’s why he never offered me any. Besides, I had that cup at the doctor’s house, remember?”

"Oh yes, while the doctor was wrapping your ribs. Are you sure you're warm enough?"

Honoria glanced around the room and smiled in amusement. "We're inside now, Mr. Comfort—I'm quite warm. But thank you for asking."

He took another sip, then quietly sat back in his chair and admired her. "You ride well. For a woman."

Her eyes narrowed. "I'd like to see you ride sidesaddle at a full run."

He held up his free hand and shook his head, chuckling all the while. "I won't argue on that, Miss Cooke. You are clearly the better rider, at least as far as sidesaddles go."

"I can ride astride as well as any man," she said matter-of-factly.

"You know, I have no doubt of that—perhaps you can show me one day. That is, if your father doesn't lock you in your room for the next decade."

"No thanks to you," she grumbled. She sat quietly for a moment, her hands in her lap, then without looking at him asked, "What are you going to do about Miss Lynch?"

"That's really none of your business, is it?"

She shrugged as she glanced up. "You looked after my welfare today, Mr. Comfort. I'm looking out for yours."

Her words warmed him and he had to smile. "Thank you, Miss Cooke—I appreciate your concern. But don't fret, I can handle Miss Lynch."

She nodded. "I'm sure you can."

He studied her a moment. There was something in her voice that gave him pause. She wasn't jealous, was she? *Hmmm.* "Perhaps I'll have lunch with her tomorrow and find out how she likes Clear Creek."

She swallowed hard but said nothing.

"I'll have to speak with her father, of course…"

"Her father?" she said. "Whatever for?"

"To see if he's going to stay around. After all, if his daughter is, I would think he'd want to as well. But one never knows."

She stiffened, her expression flat. "Of course, you're right. Why wouldn't he want to stay?"

"But then, he'll have to find a place to live—unless he plans to reside in the hotel." He examined a fingernail, then took another sip of coffee, awaiting her reaction.

"And where do you suppose Miss Lynch will live?" she asked boldly. There was a fierceness to her gaze.

He met it head-on over the rim of his cup. "I'm sure I have no idea."

She began to twist her hands in her lap, noticed she was doing it and stopped. She made it a point to look at anything in the parlor but him. "I suppose you wouldn't," she said, tightlipped.

Yes indeed, he thought to himself, *she* is *jealous!* Well, he supposed if their situations were reversed and some dandy showed up in town claiming to be her groom, he might feel the same.

Major set the cup and saucer on a nearby table and looked at Honoria, really looked at her, though she still made a show of not looking at him. She was a brushfire in a blue calico dress, full of spirit and life. Untamable. He almost licked his lips at the thought. Such a woman was rare. In the South, she'd hardly be considered wife material—too wild, too unrefined. But he wasn't in the South anymore, was he?

"What are you staring at?" she asked.

Major's eyes flicked to the dining room. Jefferson sat at the head of the table, watching them. "Well…you," he finally said.

Now it was her turn to study him, and he wondered

what could be going through her mind. “What were you just thinking about?” she blurted.

No use lying now. “Also you.”

She sighed and looked away. “I can only imagine.”

“Rest assured, it was nothing bad.”

She met his gaze. “I find that hard to believe.” She brushed a stray wisp of hair from her face. “I would think you’re still upset I won.”

He laughed. “That again?”

“Did ya?” Jefferson called from the dining room. “Did ya win?”

“Yes, Grandpa!” Honoria called back. “Of course I did!”

“That’s my gal!”

Honoria, he thought to himself. What a beautiful name. Too bad it would be improper to use it at present. He could at least think of her as Honoria in his mind.

“You’re doing it again.” She pointed at him.

“Doing?” he said with a shrug. “Doing what?”

“That funny look on your face. Like you’re up to no good.”

He pointed at himself. “Me? No good? Don’t be absurd, Miss Cooke.” He smiled slyly. “Oh, if I was truly up to no good, I’m sure you’d know.”

She leaned back in her chair. “How so?”

He wagged a finger at her. “Ah-ah-ah. I’d rather you see for yourself than have me tell you.”

She leaned forward again. “I dare you.”

Major laughed. She was so adorably unconventional! “You *are* asking for trouble, you know?”

“Oh, she knows!” Jefferson called from the dining room.

“Grandpa!” she said in shock. “Don’t encourage him!”

Jefferson’s laughter mixed with Major’s. “I like your grandfather,” he said.

"That's not surprising. The two of you are a lot alike."

"Really? How so?"

She narrowed her eyes at him and was about to comment when the front door opened, followed by the sound of booted feet. "Uh-oh," she whispered.

"Your father, I take it?" Major mouthed, motioning with his head toward the noise.

Honoria nodded nervously, her eyes glued to the foyer. She swallowed hard and said, "Hello, Papa."

Chapter Seven

"Hello, sweetling," Harrison Cooke said as he entered the parlor, his brother Colin right behind. Then he stopped short—Colin just avoiding a collision—and stared at Major. "Mr. Comfort. I was wondering whose horse that was outside. Whatever are you doing here?" He looked the room over. "In my parlor." His eyes then fixed on Honoria. "With my daughter."

"Your daughter had an accident, sir, and I wanted to make sure she got home safely," Major said without hesitation. "Your lovely wife invited me to supper."

"Accident?" Harrison and Colin said at once. They looked at each other, then at Major. "What happened?" Harrison asked as his eyebrows rose. "And don't leave anything out!"

Major noticed Honoria sink a little in her chair. He opened his mouth to speak.

But he was cut off. "Not you, Mr. Comfort." Harrison aimed his narrowed gaze at his daughter. "You. You start."

Honoria swallowed hard. "I...ah..." She took a deep breath, then was off like a shot, apparently wanting to get it over with. "I challenged Mr. Comfort to a race, took off out of town, let him catch up to me, took off again, and my horse got spooked by a fox, I fell from the saddle, but Mr. Comfort picked me up and took me to Doc Drake, who said I had a few bruised ribs and patched me up, then Mr. Comfort brought me home as he said." She stopped and caught her breath.

Harrison closed his eyes, shook his head, opened them. "You did *what*?" Colin, meanwhile, pressed his lips together and turned away to try and keep from laughing. He finally walked over to the settee and sat, doing his best to keep a straight face.

Honoria watched him and turned back to her father. "Nothing serious, really."

Major watched as Harrison's eyes grew dark. "Really? Then what is *that man* doing here?" He pointed at Major, his eyes never leaving his daughter's.

She licked her lips and sat up straighter. "If you must know, it's my fault."

Colin snorted. "That's a surprise."

"Quiet, brother," Harrison ordered. "Go on, Honoria."

She shrugged. "I challenged him to the race. What more can I say?"

"And you were injured?" Harrison's eyes narrowed further.

"Just a few bruised ribs…"

"Oh, *just* a few bruised ribs!"

"Papa," Honoria said with a roll of her eyes, "I'm fine."

"Bruised ribs, young lady, do not make you fine!" He spun to Major. "And you! What hand did you have in this?"

"I tried to stop her," he said, his eyes leveled at him. "Your daughter's reckless riding habits were the cause of the accident, I'm afraid." He glanced apologetically at Honoria, but she was nodding firmly. She was prepared to take the heat.

Harrison's jaw twitched, twice, as he glared at his

daughter. "Do you realize you could've been killed?! Good Lord, when are you going to grow up? You could have gotten yourself in a great deal of trouble! If not for Mr. Comfort here, who knows where you'd be right now?"

"Coyote fodder, no doubt," Colin tossed in.

"Uncle Colin," Honoria hissed, "you're not helping."

"Quite right. I think I'll go see what's for supper." Colin hopped off the settee and headed for the kitchen.

Harrison, his glare still fixed on his daughter, picked up where he left off. "You could be out there right now, lying half dead in the dirt!"

"I'm not lying in the dirt, Papa—I'm sitting here in the parlor talking to you. And not much the worse for wear."

"Except for the bruised ribs, of course," Major added.

Honoria gave him a pleading look, one that clearly said, *don't make this worse!*

He shrugged. "Sorry."

"And you!" Harrison once again pointed a finger at him. "You probably encouraged her!"

Major's expression went flat. He'd had about enough of this for one day, and whether he knew it or not, Harrison Cooke had crossed a line. "Dear sir, I assure you that I did nothing of the kind. And I don't believe gentlemen should make such accusations without evidence. Perhaps if your daughter wasn't such a wildcat, she wouldn't get herself in these fixes."

"What did you call her?" Harrison asked through clenched teeth.

Major held up both hands. "I meant no disrespect, sir. But I have heard today from several sources that your daughter gets herself into these messes fairly often. She needs to learn to get herself out should the need arise—or, ideally, not get into them in the first place."

That seemed to calm the man somewhat. He drew in a

deep breath and blew it out. "I apologize for overstepping my bounds, and I withdraw the accusation." He turned to Honoria. "Go to your room."

"What?" she said in shock. "Papa, I am not a child!"

"I'll believe that when you stop acting like one. You take risks no normal young lady would ever think to take."

"Perhaps because I'm not normal," she said stoically. "Would you want some dull-witted run-of-the-mill daughter?"

"There are times, Honoria…" Harrison's voice carried a wave of threat. "Besides, you're the oldest. I expect you to set an example for your younger siblings."

"A boring example," she shot back.

"Boring has nothing to do with it! You're reckless, Honoria, and if you're not careful you're going to get yourself killed one of these days."

She stood and winced.

Harrison's angry expression suddenly changed to exasperated concern. "Are you all right?"

"I'm going to my room," she said through gritted teeth. She went past him to the staircase in the foyer, took one last look at Major and ascended.

"I think she'll be fine, sir," Major said. "I was there when the doctor treated her."

Harrison stared at him. "Well… I suppose that's good to hear."

Major stood. "Perhaps I'd better go."

Harrison turned and watched Honoria disappear up the stairs, obviously in pain. He shook his head. "Anything else injured?"

"Mostly her pride," he offered.

Harrison chuckled. "Her pride could use a good thrashing. Thank you, Mr. Comfort, for taking care of her."

Major picked up his hat. "My pleasure, sir. I'd keep her

off a horse for a while, at least until those ribs heal. Good evening." He turned to leave.

Not until he reached the front door did Harrison ask, "Are you sure you won't stay?"

Major's eyes drifted up the stairwell, but there was nothing to see but stairs. "I'm sure." And he left.

Honoria entered her room and headed straight for the window. She watched Major exit the house, mount his horse, turn the animal around and trot out of the barnyard.

She sighed heavily as sadness overtook her. Why did her pride always get her into such trouble? It was as if every time she tried to do something right, it turned out wrong. Most of the time it was because she got excited and ahead of herself, and this time was no different. She tried to show off by outriding Major Comfort. What sort of fool does that?

She walked over to the bed, gingerly sat, folded her hands in her lap and stared at the floor, feeling like a complete idiot. Her father was right. She needed to grow up.

She raised her head to the ceiling at the thought and closed her eyes. The problem with growing up was there were certain things in her life she didn't want to let go of. Racing her horse across the prairie was one of them. The speed was intoxicating and gave her a sense of freedom. She especially liked to do it on days like today, with the sharp tang of autumn in the air despite the warm weather. It was her favorite time of year.

She opened her eyes and went back to staring at the floor. Her father was angry, but thankfully not as angry as he could have been. If she were lucky, she'd only get stuck cleaning out the barn…

"What did you do this time?"

Honoria looked up to see her brother Maxwell standing

in the doorway. Like her, he had their parents' dark eyes and sable hair, and like her, he had a mischievous smile. "None of your business."

Maxwell laughed. "That means you did something really naughty."

She sighed. "If you must know little brother, I raced Major Comfort and won."

"That's not what Uncle Colin said down in the kitchen."

Honoria shut her eyes against his words. Figures. "And I fell off my horse."

"I heard. You okay?"

She unconsciously put a hand to her side. "Not really, but I'll live. How was your day?" she asked, changing the subject.

"Same as always. You had all the excitement. You always have all the excitement."

She chuckled. It hurt. "That's because I break the rules. Something I shouldn't do. So don't you go break any yourself, Maxwell Cooke, you hear me?"

He crossed the room and joined her on the bed. "Have you gone mad? Ma would kill me! She doesn't strike the same fear in you like she does me."

Honoria laughed, then moaned and grabbed her ribs. "Ouch." But it was true. Whereas Pa came down hard on her, Ma came down especially hard on the other three. Maxwell, at fourteen, was usually the instigator. Twelve-year-old Clinton was the peacemaker, and Savannah, ten, the prankster. Throw in their cousins and trouble was sure to ensue. Speaking of which… "Where is everyone? Are they coming for supper tonight?"

"Jeff's still out in the barn feeding the horses. Adele's downstairs helping Ma and Aunt Belle. The rest are still at the other house."

Honoria nodded. Most nights the entire family gathered

for supper, and what a gathering it was. Between their parents and aunt and uncle, there were nine children. Toss in Grandpa Jefferson and Grandma Edith and you had quite a houseful.

"What sort of punishment did Pa give you this time?" Maxwell asked.

"He just told me to go to my room. I'm sure he'll tell me at supper." She picked at a hangnail.

"What did Mr. Comfort think?"

Her eyes darted to him as she gasped.

Maxwell's own eyes lit with interest. "That bad, huh?"

"Oh, who cares what he thinks?" Honoria said as she tenderly touched her ribs. "You'd better go wash up for supper."

"So should you," he pointed out.

Her hand moved to her belly. "I'm not really hungry. I might stay up here. Besides, Pa didn't tell me I could leave my room."

Maxwell laughed. "You're not Savannah. He probably only told you that to get you away from that man. Uncle Colin said they caught you in the parlor with him."

"Caught us in the parlor? Oh for Heaven's sake, Grandpa was chaperoning us the entire time. And 'that man's' name is Mr. Comfort, silly."

"You know Pa thinks you're too young to court."

"Maxwell, when I turn fifty, Pa will still think I'm too young to court."

Max laughed and hopped off the bed. "I'll see you downstairs." He left, closing the door behind him.

Good. She wanted a moment alone with her thoughts. Really, she wanted to relive, if only in her mind, the time she'd spent with Major on his horse, and at Doc Drake's, and on the ride home. Even their bantering in the parlor she'd hold dear.

"Oh land sakes," Honoria muttered. "So what if I do like him?" In all honesty, she was way past liking him. But what could she do about it?

Three weeks later...

"Try not to lift anything when we get there," Harrison warned as he helped Honoria down from the wagon. Thanksgiving had come and gone, and it was the first time she'd been allowed to come to Clear Creek since her "accident." She'd been bored out of her mind the whole time. She knew she was being punished, and her father was being overprotective. But she saw no reason to protect her from Major—the man was harmless as far she could tell.

Of course, perhaps her father was trying to protect her from herself most of all. She'd gotten several lectures on how to be a lady from both parents and Uncle Colin. Aunt Belle even thought she might do with a few new dresses that "befit her age," whatever that meant. For Heaven's sake, her mother and aunt didn't dress any differently than she did.

Once her feet touched the ground, she nodded her thanks and turned toward the mercantile. The absolute worst part of being stuck at the ranch the last several weeks was not hearing any news regarding Miss Lynch! If there was ever a good time to run into Fanny Fig—a debatable proposition—now would be it.

But before she could take a step, her father's hand was on her shoulder. "Here, you take care of the list. I have to see Chase at the livery stable. I'll meet you back here, then we'll go to the hotel for lunch. Oh, and see if they have some fabric for a dress," he added over his shoulder as he headed down the boardwalk. "You could do with a new one."

She nodded, put the list in her reticule and turned toward the mercantile steps. In her opinion, she needed another new dress like a hole in the head, but maybe it was his attempt to be nice after keeping her at the ranch all this time. Who could tell? She made a mental note to tell him she couldn't find a suitable cloth and trotted up the steps.

She was about to go in when someone opened the door from the inside. "Major!" she said without thinking, then snapped her mouth shut. *Oh dear...*

"Miss Cooke," he said with a smile and a tip of his hat. If he noticed her use of his Christian name, he didn't let on. "How are your ribs?"

"Much better, thank you," she said. "Good as new."

"Good enough for another race?"

Was he joking? She looked at him and smiled. "I am told that ladies do not race." She went to move past him.

He blocked her path, putting a hand on either side of the door frame. "No, they don't." He leaned down toward her ear. "Unless absolutely necessary. Not many ladies can ride like you, Miss Cooke. In an emergency it's good to know that you can." He straightened.

She looked up and their eyes locked. "Do you mean that?"

"I certainly do."

"Well...thank you. But I'm not sure if you should tell that to my father."

He leaned down again. "I'll let you in on a little secret, Miss Cooke. I think he's glad you can ride the way you do. If you were my daughter, I know I would be."

She smiled in relief. At least he didn't think her some sort of hellion.

"Oh, Majorrrrrrr!" a woman called shrilly from inside.

Honoria watched his shoulders slump and his face droop. She tried to look past him, but she already knew who was calling his name. He stepped aside and, sure enough, Miss Lucretia Lynch hurried over and grabbed his arm. "Major honey, come look at this fabric! Why, it's just about the prettiest thing I ever did see."

A chill went up Honoria's spine as she watched the woman pull him from the door. But his eyes never left hers until he was forced to turn as he followed Miss Lynch to a display table stacked with bolts of fabric. That was a good sign…she hoped.

She stood and watched the pair until the sound of the noon stage caught her attention. She turned and waved as Willie the stage driver pulled up in front of the mercantile and brought his team to a stop. He had a huge grin on his face, and she hoped he had some mail for the ranch—maybe even a letter from Uncle Duncan and Aunt Cozette. She finally stepped inside but left the door open for Willie.

"Well, if it ain't Honoria!" Grandma Waller said as she watched her approach the counter. "Welcome back."

"Hello, Grandma," Honoria said as she watched Miss Lynch giggle, still latched onto Major's arm like a prison iron. She tried not to be sick and looked at Mr. Dunnigan instead. "Willie just pulled up."

Wilfred checked his watch. "Huh. He's late. That doesn't happen often."

Grandma shrugged. "It's not like we're waiting for anything special to arrive."

"Not even me?" a man called from the doorway. Honoria looked up at the unfamiliar voice, to see an unfamiliar man standing there.

But he wasn't unfamiliar to Wilfred, who immediately gasped. "Great jumpin' Jehoshaphat, what are you doing here?"

"Isn't it obvious?" The man took a few steps forward. He was huge, very well-dressed and spoke with an accent. His eyes locked on Grandma. "Aren't you going to say hello?"

Honoria watched in shock as Grandma's lower lip trembled. She sobbed, "Why you…you old polecat! Ya never write! We hain't heard from…from you in ages, then ya go and…" She stopped, overwhelmed by her tears.

The man approached and opened his arms wide. "I wanted to surprise you."

"Andel Berg, you surprised me all right! I'm surprised ya didn't give me a heart attack!" Grandma ran into his arms and wrapped her own around his waist, resting her head against his broad chest.

"I missed you too, Grandma!" He lifted her off her feet, spun a full circle and began to laugh himself silly.

"Mr. Berg…" Honoria whispered in recollection, a smile on her face. *The* Mr. Berg?!

Footsteps stomped down the stairs behind the curtain. "Uh-oh! You're in trouble now!" Wilfred laughed.

"Who's that?" Irene Dunnigan barked as she came down the stairs. "Who's down there?" She burst through the curtains, stopped and gasped as her hands flew to her mouth. To everyone's amazement she didn't say another word, but launched herself at the giant. Once she had her arms around him, she joined Grandma in weeping—something Honoria had never seen her do.

But then, Honoria had never seen Andel Berg, former royal guardsman, former Clear Creek blacksmith, now Prince Consort of the Kingdom of Dalrovia, come to town. She'd only heard the stories. And as she watched him hug the two old women, a happy smile on his ruggedly handsome face, she suspected that all the stories were true.

Chapter Eight

When Andel finally let the women go, Wilfred came around the counter. "Tarnation, but it's good to see you!" He hugged Mr. Berg then looked past him to the door. "Where's Maddie?"

"Outside, bossing everyone around. I'll go get her."

"No need, I'll do it." Wilfred laughed and went outside.

Honoria stood and stared. Her mother described Mr. Berg to look as if he'd been carved out of marble and he certainly did. His golden hair was shoulder length, his jaw laced with golden stubble. Mr. Berg noticed her staring at him. His piercing blue eyes glinted with surprise. "You seem familiar, young lady. Should I know you?"

Grandma slapped his arm. "That there's little Honoria Cooke!"

Mr. Berg took a step back. "Harrison's daughter? I've not seen you since your parents brought you to Europe as a babe."

Honoria curtsied. "How do you do, Your Highness?"

The big man burst out laughing. "Oh, none of that 'Your Highness' here—if you're a Cooke, you're family. And I'm doing very well, except I'm hungry." He looked at

Mrs. Dunnigan. "Any chance you've made that famous pot roast of yours?"

"Just happen to have one in the oven," she said through her tears and hugged him again.

Honoria noticed Major and Miss Lynch were staring at the scene, just as fascinated.

Mr. Berg finally noticed them. "And whom might you be?"

"Major Quincy Comfort, at your service sir."

Mr. Berg bowed. "Andel Berg, at yours." He straightened. "And the lady?"

Miss Lynch gripped Major's arm tighter, making him wince. "Miss Lucretia Lynch." She stared at him, obviously trying to make sense of his recent words with Honoria. Finally she said, "My, what a funny little accent you have!"

"Indeed," Mr. Berg replied. And he did, but Honoria knew he would. He was of some sort of Scandinavian descent, she recalled.

The bell above the door rang and Wilfred re-entered, a pretty blonde-haired woman on his arm. "Look who I found outside!"

Grandma and Mrs. Dunnigan left Mr. Berg for the newcomer, throwing their arms around her and speaking at once. "Maddie!" And the waterworks started all over again.

"Why can't they do that outside?" Miss Lynch objected. "Such emotional displays are hardly dignified!"

"You'll have to excuse us, ma'am," Wilfred said. "We hain't seen the Bergs in years. In fact, this is the first time they've set foot in Clear Creek like normal folks since they left us back in '59."

"Like…normal folks?" Miss Lynch repeated, still confused.

Grandma and Mrs. Dunnigan let go of Maddie. Honoria watched as she joined her husband and gave him a hug. "It's good to be back," she said. Honoria smiled at their height difference—Queen Madelaina Van Zuyen barely came up to her husband's chest.

Mrs. Dunnigan wiped away her tears. "Don't you go away—I'm gonna run upstairs and check on that pot roast!"

"We wouldn't think of it," Mr. Berg said with a smile.

"Land sakes, I gotta find Doc!" Grandma cried. "He'll want to know you're here!"

Mr. Berg laughed. "We'll come by the house for a visit, I promise. I've missed your cookies."

Grandma held Maddie's hand and gave it a squeeze. "I'll start a batch for him right away." She kissed the younger woman on the cheek and hurried from the mercantile, tears in her eyes.

"Well, *we* really must be going," Miss Lynch said, trying to pull Major toward the door.

But all she succeeded in doing was losing her death-grip on his arm. Taking advantage of his new-found freedom, he went over to Honoria. "How are you?"

Honoria's eyes darted between the two. "Very well, thank you." She fixed her gaze on him. "And you?" She was afraid to ask, but did it anyway. So much for the need to find Fanny Fig to obtain information—it was obvious the pair were courting.

"I'm well," he said, his eyes locked on hers as he rubbed the feeling back into his arm.

Miss Lynch sighed in annoyance and pretended to study the goods behind the counter.

"And your brothers?" Honoria asked, if only to keep him talking. Maybe she'd find out if they'd set a wedding date.

"They're all fine. Michael and Darcy are in town, down at the livery stable."

"So is my father. I'm sure they've said hello." She glanced at the Bergs, who along with Wilfred were watching them with interest.

"Major!" Miss Lynch said with a frown. "We really must be going!"

"You can go on if you'd like," he replied, not even looking at her. "You know the way back to the hotel."

Her mouth dropped open as she gasped. "Well, I never! What has gotten into you?" She looked at Honoria, then muttered, "I see. Well, I'll just wait for you at the hotel, then. I'm sure you're not so *ungentlemanly* as to cancel your lunch with Daddy and me."

He still didn't glance at her. "Of course not. If you must know, Miss Cooke took a horrible fall a few weeks ago and I wanted to know how she's doing."

"She just *told* you how she's doing. What else did you want to know?"

He finally looked—*glared*—her way. "I don't see how that's any of your concern."

Mr. Berg shifted his weight and crossed his arms over his chest, still listening with interest. He looked at each of them in turn and arched an eyebrow.

Honoria hoped the giant didn't butt in. "I don't want to keep you if you have somewhere you need to be," she told Major.

"You're not keeping me from anything important," he said.

"Not important!" Miss Lynch huffed. "Major Comfort! You...you...oh, forget it! I'll see you at the hotel!" She went to the door and turned, one hand on the knob. "And don't be late!" She left, slamming the door behind her.

"Patience is not one of that woman's virtues, is it?" Mr.

Berg stated to no one in particular. He smiled at his wife, kissed the top of her head and turned back to Honoria and Major. It was clear he didn't mind reminding them that they had an audience.

Honoria begin to fidget. "Perhaps I'd better go too. I have to meet my father."

"You ain't given me your list yet," Wilfred pointed out. "You did come in here to buy something, didn't you?"

Honoria closed her eyes and held her breath. Could she have made herself look any more foolish? Well, probably, but better not to think about it. She opened her eyes and reached into her reticule as she turned back to the counter. "Sorry, Wilfred."

He chuckled and took the paper from her hand. "I'll get right on this." He looked at them. "Don't stop talking on my account."

"Heaven forbid," Major said. He glanced at the Bergs, then turned back to Honoria, looking much more relaxed now that Miss Lynch had departed. "We're getting along, my brothers and I. Pleasant is in town as well—she should be here any minute."

"Good, I'd love to see her. I haven't been in town for quite some time."

He lowered his voice. "Your punishment?"

She felt her cheeks grow hot. "You could say that."

"I'm sorry. I guess this means there's no chance for a rematch."

She giggled and shook her head. "My poor father would have a heart attack."

Major's eyes flicked once more to the Bergs and back. "Are they going to stand there and watch us the entire time?"

"I think they're just being polite."

"I think they're being nosy," he whispered with a low chuckle. "Who are they?"

"Close friends of my family. They'll probably be at the ranch tomorrow. My father's going to be so excited when he sees them."

"Now there's something I'd like to witness," he said with a smile.

She smiled shyly, feeling ten years old again. "Mr. Berg is kind of famous in these parts."

"Famous?" he said, his voice barely above a whisper again. "How so? What did he do?"

Wilfred leaned over the counter. "He was the blacksmith," he whispered. "And he can probably hear you."

Major and Honoria both glanced at Mr. Berg, who stood, a happy smile on his face. He nodded and grinned in acknowledgment. Major straightened, went to him and offered his hand. Mr. Berg took it and gave it a healthy shake. "I hope you don't mind my checking on Miss Cooke's welfare," he said.

"Not at all. I can see you are concerned over her."

"Have you lived here long?" Maddie asked. Honoria noticed her accent as well, but that was to be expected.

"Only since last spring," Major explained.

"Him and his five brothers," Wilfred tossed in.

"Five?" Mrs. Berg said with raised eyebrows.

"They all live at the men's camp outside of town," Wilfred continued.

Major glanced over his shoulder. "I'm perfectly capable of informing Mr. and Mrs. Berg of my affairs, Mr. Dunnigan."

"Just trying to help," Wilfred chuckled.

"So you've settled here," Mr. Berg said. "You and your brothers must like Clear Creek."

Major glanced over his shoulder again, this time at Honoria. She blushed and started to shop around the mercantile. "Yes," he said. "We do like it here. Clear Creek is a nice little town."

"That it is," Mr. Berg agreed. "I'm sure we'll be seeing you around. I look forward to meeting your brothers."

"We'd best take care of business," his wife said.

"Yes, I suppose so. Wilfred?"

"Yes?"

"We have some business to take care of at the hotel but will be back in time for supper." Mr. Berg looked up at the ceiling and said loudly, "Tell your lovely wife I can't wait to enjoy her pot roast again!"

"I heard that!" came a muffled reply from above.

Mr. Berg laughed, bowed, turned to his wife and headed toward the door.

But before they could open it, Paddy Mulligan came bursting through. "Bless me soul, it's true! Ye really are here!"

"Mr. Mulligan!" Mr. Berg released his wife and let the other man hug him.

Mr. Berg smiled as they slapped each other on the back, Mr. Mulligan grunting each time. "It's good to see you."

Mr. Mulligan took a few steps back, coughing. "Not half as good as it is to see ye." He turned. "Maddie!" Mr. Mulligan pulled her into his arms and hugged her as well, sans the slapping. "What a sight for sore eyes ye are. Wait until the Missus sees ye." He looked up at Mr. Berg. "She's baking pies today," he said with an exaggerated wink then glanced around. "Have ye brought the wee ones with ye?"

"No, not on trips like this," Mr. Berg said. "Perhaps when they're older."

"We're sorry, Mr. Mulligan," Maddie added. "Maybe next time."

Mr. Mulligan sighed. "I understand. And gratified to know there *will be* a next time!"

The Bergs nodded and gave Mr. Mulligan another hug. "Wilfred?" Mr. Berg said.

"I understand. You get your business at the hotel taken care of and I'll see you later. How about I invite Doc and Grandma?"

"And me and the Missus?" Mr. Mulligan asked, hopeful.

Wilfred rolled his eyes. "Oh, all right."

The others laughed as Maddie smiled. "That would be wonderful. It will be a nice visit with all of you."

Mr. Berg guided his wife to the door alongside Mr. Mulligan who began chatting about the saloon. Once they left, the mercantile fell into silence.

Major and Honoria stared at each other a moment or two as Wilfred gazed longingly at the door. After a moment he straightened, wiped a tear from his eye and returned to work.

"Wilfred?" Honoria said. "Are you all right?"

"Got dust in my eye is all. You two go back to doing whatever it was you were doing."

"Well," Major said. "There are interruptions, and then there are interruptions."

"Mr. Berg was hardly an interruption," Honoria said. "Everyone in town will be talking about this. There'll probably be a big party at the saloon or hotel this week."

"A party?" Major said in surprise. "For the old blacksmith and his wife? Wait…you did say something about 'Your Highness'…"

Wilfred snorted in amusement behind the counter but continued to fill Honoria's order.

"Yes, he's not just a blacksmith." She took a moment to think. "Well, it's rather a long story. The short version is, he was a palace guard who lived here as a smith before I was born. But he'd been sent here to keep an eye on Maddie, who didn't know she was the heir to the throne of this little country in Europe called Dalrovia. While he was here, he helped rescue my aunts, Mrs. Dunnigan and my mother from some outlaws. He and Maddie married—that's a whole other story in itself—and now she's a queen and he's her consort. But I guess things are going well enough back home that they could afford the time to visit here again."

"Is that so?" Major rubbed his forehead in surprise. "That is quite a story. Do you often get such…odd occurrences around here?"

"I suppose we do. My uncle Duncan inherited a duchy in England—my father and Uncle Colin can tell you all about that. There's the Scotsman and his wife who show up now and then…"

"That would be Mr. MacDonald," Wilfred said as he continued his work. "Ain't seen him around since Duncan and Cozette came to visit the first time. Tarnation, that had to be back when Newton got married."

"Newton Whitman Holmes," Honoria elaborated. "You're right, that's when I met them. There was an African couple who came through a couple of times—not just Negroes, but actually from Africa. And of course, the time a mail-order bride arrived in town followed by her six brothers—that was a little odd too," she added with a smile.

Major laughed at that, then stopped. "Newton Whitman Holmes… I've heard the name before, but I've never met the man."

"He and his wife Arya moved to England. They live with Duncan and Cozette now. So do Amon and Nettie Cotter—Nettie is Newton's sister. Their father, Cutty Holmes, still lives in the area."

Major glanced between them. "I knew this town had a heavy British influence, but is everyone planning to move to England?" He smiled wryly, indicating he was joking.

Honoria laughed. "I can't imagine living anywhere but America. I'd love to visit England one day—I haven't been since I was baby—but I don't see it happening any time soon."

"A trip like that would be lovely," Major said as he gazed into her eyes.

It was all Honoria could do not to fidget. "I suppose you shouldn't keep Miss Lynch and her father waiting," she said.

He sighed in resignation. "No, I suppose I shouldn't. I have things to discuss with Mr. Lynch."

Honoria's heart sank. He needed to talk to him about the wedding, no doubt. She swallowed hard and nodded. "You'd best get on, then."

He leaned toward her, his head dropping toward hers. "Promise me something."

Her eyes met his again. "What?"

"That you'll not go racing across the prairie without me."

Honoria's heart stopped. What was he saying? Come to think of it, why say anything, especially if he was going to marry Miss Lynch?

"I'd hate to think of anything happening to you when you're by yourself," he said.

Oh—he just wanted to warn her not to go acting like a fool again. She forced a smile and nodded. "Don't worry, I won't."

"I'm gratified to hear that. Now if you'll excuse me, Miss Lynch is nothing if not impatient."

"I noticed," she said.

With a tip of his hat, he left the mercantile. For Honoria, he might as well have been leaving Clear Creek. Now she wanted to cry—and not for joy as Grandma and Mrs. Dunnigan had.

Chapter Nine

Honoria trudged towards the livery stable. Wilfred had long since filled her order, and she'd gotten tired of waiting for her father to show up. No doubt he'd run into Mr. Berg and they were catching up on old times.

Several people ran past her as she walked, hurrying toward the other end of town. Even Bowen Drake and his wife Ellie ran by, not bothering to even shout hello. It was amazing how one couple could cause such a stir. But then, the Bergs were no ordinary couple. She might as well join the melee and see if she could find her father in the growing crowd.

When she reached the livery stable there was a huge group of people outside and more coming. For Heaven's sake, how would she find him in this mess?

"Honoria!" Uncle Colin shouted. He fought his way out and took her hand. "Stay close to me. Your father's in the middle of all this."

"Where exactly is the middle?" she shouted above the throng yelling and calling out greetings to the Bergs.

"I'm not sure," Uncle Colin yelled back. "But if we keep moving, we'll get there. I dare say, over half the town is here!"

He was right—almost everyone she knew was gathered between the livery stable and the hotel, all angling for position to get to the Bergs. She caught sight of Darcy Comfort, who shrugged as if to say *what's all this about?* She smiled in return. He'd find out for himself—or maybe Major would fill him in. Her earlier heartbreak over discovering Major and Miss Lynch's courtship was being assuaged by the excitement of the Bergs' return to Clear Creek. She gripped Uncle Colin's hand as he pushed his way through the crowd.

A booming laugh could be heard, followed by her father's voice. "Any word from Duncan?"

"We've not seen them lately," Mr. Berg answered loudly.

"We hope to visit them when we return," she heard Maddie yell.

"All right, all right, give 'em some breathin' room!" Eli Turner shouted over the din. "What're ya folks tryin' to do, crush 'em?"

People began to back up, which helped Colin and Honoria break through. "Finally!" Colin whispered, then took one look at Mr. Berg and let out a very un-English "Whoopee! Andel Berg, as I live and breathe! How are you, old chap?"

Mr. Berg pulled Colin into a fierce embrace and slapped him on the back, much as he had Mr. Mulligan, eliciting a similar grunt from her uncle. "Colin, so good to see you! Maddie, look, it's Colin!"

"Colin!" Maddie hugged Honoria's uncle. She wished her mother and aunt were here—they were missing out on all the excitement.

Sheriff Tom Turner shoved his way through the crowd. "Is it true?" He stopped short when he saw Mr. Berg and his jaw went slack. "Land sakes, it is!" He cocked his head to one side as if he'd expected to see something else.

Mr. Berg perused him in the same way. "Little Tommy Turner?" he boomed. The crowd quieted in response and stepped further away to give them more room. Mr. Berg put his hands on his hips and looked Tom Turner up and down in amazement. "You're the sheriff now?"

"'Course I am," Tom said. He looked at Harrison. "Just what do ya put in them letters ya send these people? Don't ya tell 'em nothin'?"

"You haven't been sheriff long enough for me to write about it," Harrison said, clearly flustered. "It's only been over a year now. Besides, I thought Colin told them."

"I thought you did," Colin replied in shock.

"Shoot—I guess I should've done it myself," Tom said with a shake of his head. "Well, it don't matter—Mr. Berg figgered it out."

"I'm sure you make a good sheriff, Tom," Mr. Berg said with a smile. "And who is your deputy over there?"

"That there's my little brother Eli," Tom said proudly.

"Eli?" Mr. Berg said in surprise.

"He couldn't have been more than seven when we left," Maddie said.

Mr. Berg's eyes fell on Honoria. "All the little ones have grown up." He looked over the crowd, which had gone silent. He suddenly smiled, raised his hands in the air and yelled, "It's good to be back!"

Everyone cheered, Honoria included. At least having the Bergs in town would give her something else to think about. She didn't want to waste all her time fretting over Major Comfort. She'd thought about him far too much during her…incarceration. And to what end? He wasn't even here, as far as she could tell—probably still at the hotel with Miss Lynch and her father. Time for her to move on. She launched herself into the Bergs' arms.

"You will, of course, come to supper!" she heard her father say.

"Tomorrow," Mr. Berg said. "Tonight we have been promised Mrs. Dunnigan's pot roast!" The crowd went wild.

"I bet I know what else ye're looking forward to!" Mr. Mulligan shouted. "Pie!"

Honoria could hardly believe it—the people got even louder as they cheered and laughed in response! Then she remembered that Mr. Berg had helped make Clear Creek famous for pie—and why. She giggled to herself, and hoped that Pleasant had the opportunity to meet the couple while they were visiting. Ma and Aunt Belle had teased poor Pleasant relentlessly about the use of pie while she was courting Eli. She glanced around, but didn't see her in the crowd either.

She swallowed hard as tears stung the back of her eyes. Pleasant and Eli were happily married, as were so many others. And she…she unconsciously glanced toward the hotel, but with so many people surrounding her, she couldn't see it. She wished she could disappear through the crowd and go home, but there was no way to escape easily. Perhaps if she worked her way backward, she could go find someplace to sit and be miserable while her father and uncle visited. She could always speak with the Bergs when they came to the ranch for supper tomorrow evening.

She slowly stepped back and did her best to worm her way through the crushing throng. After several minutes, she was finally able to break free, turned…and found herself facing the hotel. It figured. She took a deep breath, free from the pushing and shoving, and headed toward it for lack of a better idea.

In the hotel lobby, Lorcan Brody raised his head from behind the counter as she walked toward him. "Don't tell me…let me try to get it right. Not Sadie…not Belle…but definitely from the Triple-C, that I can tell. Honoria?"

She shook her head in wonder. "How do you do that?"

He smiled. "Years of practice. Besides, ye all have the same scent—it's that fancy English soap the Duke sends ye."

"Oh, so that's what gives us away."

"At least the ladies," he said. "Duncan sends yer father and uncle a different kind."

"Yes, he does." She leaned over the counter. "And just to let you know, we plan to give some to the Kincaids for Christmas this year. You'll try not to get us all confused, won't you?"

Lorcan laughed, his sightless eyes moving this way and that. "It'll be a challenge, but I'll get ye all sorted out."

"I'm sure you will—you always do." She looked toward the dining parlor. She couldn't see Major or the Lynches, but could hear their voices.

"Looking for someone?" Lorcan asked.

She sighed. "No, I just thought I'd get away from the crowd outside. I'm sure you've met Mr. Berg by now."

"No, I haven't—they've not gotten this far. But I met their secretary and associates."

"Associates?"

"Yes, they've checked into the hotel and are upstairs preparing the rooms. They are…very different. They smell…spicy."

Honoria laughed. "Probably because they come from Dalrovia."

"Ah, that would explain the accents too. Mr. Van Cleet told me once where the Bergs were from, but I admit I'd forgotten. I look forward to meeting them. And I'm sure Ada would love to ask them a few things."

"Wouldn't we all?" She turned and stared out the hotel's

front windows at the crowd beyond. "How many people are they traveling with?"

"At least half a dozen, mostly men," Lorcan said. "They had to have escorted the stage on horseback. They couldn't have ridden inside."

"My goodness," Honoria said. "With such an escort, I would think so."

"Indeed. Let's see, there's what I assume to be a ladies maid, and the rest are Palace guard or some such, I imagine, considering who they are. But I know Their Majesties want to be treated like normal people while they're here. Mr. Van Cleet told me that too, in case they ever showed up."

"Yes, please do. It helps them feel more comfortable, and folks are less likely to make a fuss over them."

"You mean like now?" Lorcan said with a laugh. "Still, I know Ada and others are going to have a lot of questions. It's all rather exciting, isn't it?"

"What?" Honoria had been distracted by the voices from the dining room.

"Having them here. After all, it's not every day the hotel gets to play host to royalty. A queen and her consort, no less."

Honoria sighed and turned back to the window. "It's not every day we get visitors to Clear Creek of any kind."

"Ahem." Honoria and Lorcan turned to find Mr. Lynch at the other end of the counter. "You wouldn't happen to know where Mrs. Upton has got to? We're waiting for the next course."

"I believe she's outside greeting our new guests," Lorcan said.

"I'll fetch her for you," Honoria offered. It was time she left anyway. She didn't think she could stand to see Major sitting with Miss Lynch at lunch.

"That's very kind of you my dear," Mr. Lynch said. "Thank you so much."

Honoria left the hotel, thinking, *believe me, the pleasure is all mine.*

On the way home, her father and Colin talked and talked about Andel and Maddie Berg. How long had they been in America? Why hadn't they written and said they were coming? More than a fair share was spent on how good the couple looked. "I swear they've hardly aged a day since we last saw them last," Uncle Colin said for at least the twelfth time since leaving town.

"I know—strange, isn't it?" her father remarked.

"Maybe they eat differently in Europe," Honoria suggested from the back of the wagon as they bumped along.

Her father twisted on his seat to look at her. "Good thinking, poppet. Why else would they look so good after all these years?"

"Not to mention they're not chasing after cattle like the rest of us," Uncle Colin added.

"Yes, that too," said her father. "It must be nice to be them."

"Mama and Auntie Belle will be upset they missed them," Honoria said with a sigh.

Her father turned again. "Is something the matter?"

She swallowed hard. "No, Papa. Nothing."

He studied her a moment, then faced forward again. "Your mother and aunt will be ecstatic. Andel and Maddie will be with us for supper tomorrow evening, so I expect you children to be on your best behavior."

She smiled. "Because the rulers of Dalrovia are dining with us?"

"No, because your mother will use her best china—and you know how particular she is with that set."

"As are the rest of us," Colin agreed.

Honoria nodded. The china had belonged to her namesake, her father and uncle's mother. "I'll make sure everyone is extra careful."

"See that you do," her father said. "Now, what do you suppose should be on the menu tomorrow evening?"

"Whatever they don't have in Dalrovia, I guess." She stared at the road behind them. Major was back there, probably enjoying dessert with Miss Lynch and her father. She shuddered at the thought. She would really have to work at getting that man out of her head—or be miserable until she got over him.

It was a good thing he had no idea of her feelings for him—how embarrassing would that be? Worse, what if Miss Lynch found out? Egads, who knew what she'd do? She didn't exactly come across as the caring type—more like a hardened harpy. She stifled a sob and coughed into her hand to cover it, her eyes darting to her father and uncle to make sure they hadn't noticed. Thankfully, they kept chatting between them, making plans for their supper guests tomorrow.

She sunk against the sacks of flour she was leaning against. She just wanted to get home, go to her room and have a good cry. Better yet, she wanted to saddle her horse and race across the prairie, get as far away from Clear Creek and Major Comfort as she could. Then maybe her heart wouldn't hurt so much. The more she thought about it, the worse she felt.

Of course, she had only herself to blame. That's what she got for letting herself dream of things that could never be. Besides, what did she think he saw in her? Hadn't he called her a wildcat in front of her father not weeks before? No wonder he was courting Miss Lynch—she was a refined Southern belle. Much more suitable for a Southern gentleman than a horse-racing, parent-defying frontier mongrel like herself.

Honoria sunk until she was practically lying down and stared at the sky, its bright blue in sharp contrast to the fluffy white clouds. "Please, Lord," she whispered. "Make this stop."

She had no idea seeing Major with Miss Lynch would affect her like this, but it had. Her only guess was that in all the excitement of the Bergs showing up, it hadn't had time to sink in until now. She supposed she would just have to muddle through and hope she got over it fast. Got over *him*. She rubbed her hands over her face as if doing so would wipe thoughts of Major out of her mind. But no, his face kept flashing before her, demanding to be seen.

She sat back up and took a deep breath. She'd have to get a hold of herself before they got home. Mama and Auntie Belle would want to know all about Mr. and Mrs. Berg, and even though her father and Uncle Colin would do most of the talking, they would still ask her what she thought of the couple. But she didn't want to talk about them, or about anything. If she opened her mouth, the only thing to come out of it would be her own wretched sobs, and then the worst would happen. *They'd ask her what was wrong.*

She wiped at the few tears that had managed to escape. They felt hot against her cold cheeks. What could she tell them? *I talked myself into falling in love with Major Quincy Comfort over the last three weeks and now he's going to marry that horrible Miss Lynch. And all because I made a fool of myself, and then Papa grounded me for three weeks, and that wouldn't even matter if I hadn't already proven I was so unsuitable for him and God knows who would ever want me and...*

She shut her eyes against the cataract of condemning thoughts. She knew she couldn't say a word. She'd just have to bear it alone and face the cold hard facts that she'd messed things up. Worse, it was her own thoughts that put her in her current state of distress. Maybe if she hadn't let herself dream of a life with Major over the last three weeks, she wouldn't be dealing with a broken heart today.

You're a fool, Honoria Cooke, she told herself. *You're a bloody idiot.*

Strangely, that made it easier for Honoria to push thoughts of Major Comfort from her mind. After all, he deserved better than her.

Chapter Ten

The next day was a flurry of activity at the Triple-C. Honoria's mother and aunt wanted everything to be perfect for their supper guests—and "perfect" meant a lot of work. Aunt Belle even insisted they polish the silver. After all, she explained to the children, it wasn't every day they had royalty in the house. This got the little ones excited—they'd never met the Bergs. Neither had Honoria until the previous day, but she was old enough to know of their humble beginnings.

Maddie Van Zuyen, before ascending to the Dalrovian throne, had lived with her parents in New York City before heading west in '59. Her father, a prince, and his countess wife Apollonia had fled their country, wanting nothing to do with the crown. Together they'd had a child, Madelaina, though her mother called her Madeline or Maddie for short.

While growing up, Maddie's mother worked as a headmistress at a school for girls, while her father avoided work, spending his days gambling and womanizing. It was one of the reasons they'd traveled west in the first place—the countess thought a change would help her husband to escape his bad habits. The prince was agreeable, thinking it would get him away from the Dalrovian guard sent to find him.

Unfortunately, bad habits weren't shaken so easily, and they got the prince shot on the trail. This left a horrible mark on the countess and her daughter. They were fortunate enough to join another wagon train and escape the ridicule heaped upon them by their fellow travelers. That those same fellow travelers had killed her husband didn't help, nor that they did nothing to the woman involved. Apollonia carried that bitterness with her.

Thanks to the protection and guidance of their new wagonmaster, one Dallan MacDonald, the countess and her daughter settled in Clear Creek. Mr. MacDonald and his wife suggested the small town would be a better place to put down roots than Oregon City, where people from their previous wagon train would also be settling. The countess wholeheartedly agreed, wanting to be free of the taunts and jabs, not to mention keep her and her daughter's true identities secret.

But Andel Berg, the town's new blacksmith, had a secret identity of his own—*he* was the Dalrovian guard sent to find the crown prince! With said prince dead, he was now tasked to find the next heir in line to the throne…the prince's daughter, Crown Princess Madelaina. And who should come along but Maddie Van Zuyen—who hadn't a clue she was a princess. This led to an unusual set of events, including a *literal* shotgun marriage between Andel and Maddie.

It all worked out in the end, of course. Maddie and Andel had returned to Europe to become Queen Madelaina and Prince Consort Andel, Apollonia married a French trapper (and father-in-law of the Duke of Stantham) named Anton Duprie, and they all were in the process of living happily ever after. Honoria thought it all terribly romantic and wanted to ask Maddie for more details after supper. If she could catch a few private moments with her, that is. She hoped her parents didn't monopolize the conversation during the meal...

"Are you done polishing the spoons?" Auntie Belle asked, interrupting her thoughts.

"Almost. Savannah is still working on the knives."

Her aunt looked at Honoria's younger sibling on the other side of the table and smiled. "Savannah, stop checking your teeth in the reflections and start polishing."

"But that's how I know it's done," the little girl answered. "I can see them clearly."

Honoria laughed. "I never thought of that." She smiled and checked her reflection in the back of a spoon. "You're right, it works."

"Toldja," Savannah said with a grin.

Aunt Belle put her hands on her hips and shook her head. "Just get it done. Then you can help with the pies."

"How many pies are we baking?" Honoria asked.

"Enough that Mr. Berg can take several back to the hotel with him."

"Several?" Honoria said. "Why would you want to do that? Can't Mrs. Upton bake him some...oh. It's part of that joke, isn't it? Grandma was joking yesterday about baking him pies."

"Joke? I don't get it," Savannah added.

"Never you mind." Aunt Belle scowled as she headed back to the kitchen.

"He must really like pie," Savannah said.

"Something like that." Though Honoria knew the joke was much more...adult. Otherwise, why was no one willing to explain it? And how old would she have to be before someone did?

"Should I bake him one?" Savannah asked, innocently.

Honoria had a sudden flash of the night Eli and Pleasant had pie on the porch while courting. They fell in love over that pie. It must be something along those lines. She sighed at the thought and went back to polishing spoons.

The rest of the day was spent cooking, baking and generally preparing for their guests. The children became more and more excited the closer it drew to suppertime. To them, this was like having an extra holiday between Thanksgiving and Christmas—only with more labor involved. Even the older boys were at work straightening up around the ranch houses and outbuildings.

"Who *are* these people?" Thackary, Colin and Belle's middle son, asked his younger brother Samuel as they stacked wood in a shed.

"I don't know," Sam said. "But they must be important, or Ma and Pa wouldn't be making such a fuss."

"I heard he was the blacksmith," Thackary said. "Is that true, Honoria?"

Honoria set down the wheelbarrow full of wood she'd just brought in, grabbed a few pieces and handed them to Sam. She'd needed to escape the hot kitchen and had volunteered to help the boys for a while. "Yes. But then things...happened. He got married, then wound up in a foreign country."

"Does he shoe horses over there too?" Sam asked.

"Not exactly," she said with a smile.

"Then what does he do?" Thackary this time.

"Well...he and his wife run the country."

"Is he their president?" Sam asked in awe.

"No," Honoria said. "He's their king. Sort of."

The boys' eyes widened. It was hard for them to grasp the concept of a king and queen as opposed to a president running the country. The only sort of monarchy they knew was in fairy tales.

"Why don't you ask him about it when they get here?" she suggested, glancing at the road from the barnyard. "They should be here soon." She turned back to the boys. "I'd better get back to the kitchen and take the pies out of the oven. You two finish up here."

"Do we *have* to put on our Sunday clothes?" Sam asked.

"Yes—your mother wants you to look your best."

"We don't have to dress up when Uncle Duncan comes to visit. And he's a *duke*."

"A king outranks a duke," Honoria pointed out. Not that it mattered to either of her cousins. "Now hurry up and get your chores done." She brushed dirt and woodchips from her apron and hurried back to the main ranch house. She wished she had enough time to take a bath and wash her hair, but that wasn't about to happen with all the work that still needed to be done. Instead, she'd have to settle for washing her face and calling it good.

Besides, she didn't feel the need to impress the Bergs, even if they were royalty. She'd heard so many stories about them growing up that she knew them more as a simple blacksmith and a girl from a wagon train. There wasn't a lot of mention of the whole royalty part. She *was* curious as to how Maddie's mother the countess (now Queen Mother?) was doing. After all, she ended up marrying her Aunt Cozette's father. If he married a countess, what did that make him? Was he now a count? Would a fur trapper care about such things? Hard to say.

Back in the kitchen she took the last two pies out of the oven, set them on the worktable and wiped her brow. She looked at the other nine already cooling. It was more than they'd baked at Thanksgiving!

"Is that all of them?" Honoria's mother asked as she came into the kitchen.

"Yes, thank Heaven." Honoria stretched the kinks out of her back. "I could do with a nap at this point."

"No time for that." Her mother studied the pies. "I do hope eleven is enough."

"How can it not be, Mother?"

"Andel and Maddie aren't traveling alone. There's a host of people with them."

"Oh yes, Lorcan mentioned that when I was at the hotel."

"Probably bodyguards of some sort. Soldiers, maybe." Her mother looked at her quizzically. "What were you doing at the hotel?"

Honoria suddenly took interest in one of the pies, poking it with a fork. "Just waiting for Papa." Best to steer Mama away from any mention of the hotel. She looked up. "Since when does Mr. Berg need protection? Uncle Duncan doesn't travel with anyone."

Her mother sighed. "Andel and Maddie are royalty in a different country. I suppose it's just the way things are done there."

Her words made Honoria glad she lived in Clear Creek and didn't have to deal with such nonsense. "How many more places should I set at the table?"

"I'm not sure yet. We might have to borrow your Aunt Belle's table and set it up in the parlor."

"Oh Mama, don't be ridiculous."

Her mother chewed her bottom lip, a sure sign she was worried. "I hope they're all right..."

Honoria was shocked. "For Heaven's sake, no one in town is going to try to harm Andel or Maddie! Why would they?"

"Not everyone in town knows who they are, dear. Or more importantly, *what* they are."

"And no one's going to say anything either. Besides, the

only people new in town are the Comforts, and I'm sure Eli has told Pleasant by now. I don't see any of her brothers being a problem." She swallowed hard and turned away as thoughts of Major struck. She still wasn't over seeing him the day before. Worse, her mind was now conjuring up images of Major and Miss Lynch standing at the altar in front of Preacher Jo. What a nightmare!

"Are you all right?"

Honoria jumped. "I'm fine. Just…tired. We've been working all day."

Her mother nodded and glanced around the kitchen. "Why don't you go upstairs and take a little rest after all? I'll get the biscuits in the oven. But make sure your brothers and sister are dressed properly for supper."

"I will."

Her mother turned and headed for the stove. "Oh, and Honoria?"

"Yes?"

"Why don't you wear your new pink dress? Tonight will give you a chance to show it off."

Honoria sighed as her shoulders slumped. At this point she didn't care what she wore, and the only person she wanted to show off for wasn't going to be there. "Fine."

Her mother smiled, nodded, then stared at the stove, hands on her hips, as if expecting it to put up a fight. She loved and hated that stove at the same time, Honoria knew. It was wonderful to work with, but terrible to clean.

Honoria went up to her room and flopped onto the bed. Closing her eyes, she tried to clear her mind of Major and all that had transpired between them on that fateful day. A race, a romance—at least in her mind—and a set of bruised ribs. Ah, love. Except it wasn't.

She put an arm over her eyes and sighed heavily. Maybe she ought to clean the stove to get her mind off things. She was beginning to despair of ever getting married. Not that there weren't eligible bachelors in town—on the contrary, there were plenty. But she couldn't stand the thought of having to see Major with Miss Lynch, soon to be *Mrs. Comfort*, glued to his side all the time. What torture! She'd rather be somewhere, anywhere else.

Perhaps it was time to broach the subject of visiting Uncle Duncan with her parents. Hmmm, could she get the Bergs to side with her? After all, wouldn't it broaden her mind to visit another country, live in the land of her forefathers for a time? Maybe Uncle Duncan could even find a suitable husband for her in England. Far, far away from the Comforts—and Lynches.

She sat up at the thought. "Marry an Englishman… yes, that's what I'll do. Father can't argue with that." At least, not if Uncle Duncan approved. But was Uncle Duncan as overprotective as father? Good heavens, what if he was *worse*?

Honoria fell against the pillows and groaned. "My life is a nightmare," she muttered. Maybe if she were lucky, she'd wake up soon…

"Honoria, wake up!"

Honoria bolted to a sitting position and gasped. "What?!" She glanced around, unsure of where she was at first, then realized she was in her room. "Oh good grief, what time is it?"

"Time for you to get dressed," her father said. "What have you been doing up here?"

"Napping," she said in exasperation. "Wasn't it obvious? Body prone, eyes shut…"

"Oh, never mind that," he said with a wave of his hand. "The Bergs will be here any minute. Hurry up!" He disappeared from the doorway and she listened to his retreating footsteps as he hurried downstairs. He seemed even more nervous than Mother, if that was possible.

She got up and went to the armoire in the corner and opened it. “Where’s my pink dress?” She rifled through her clothes but there was no sign of the frock. “Where on earth…oh!” She slapped her palm against her forehead. Her cousin Adele had wanted to try it on, and had probably taken it home to do so. That meant she had to go next door to fetch it. “Land sakes, doesn’t anyone return anything around here?”

She continued to grumble as she marched down the stairs, out the front door and straight to her aunt and uncle’s house, going in without knocking. Sam and Thackary were in the parlor in their Sunday best, each with a book in their hands. “What are you doing here?” Thackary asked.

“Adele has one of my dresses. I’m here to get it back.” She headed for the staircase. The second ranch house had much the same layout as the main one, only the rooms weren’t as big.

“You mean that pink one?” Thackary called after her.

Honoria stopped mid-stair, bending over the banister to see back into the parlor. “Yes, what about it?”

“Adele’s wearing it,” Sam said.

“What! She can’t wear that dress! *I’m* wearing it.”

The boys tossed their books to the side and raced out of the parlor to the staircase. “Oh boy, Honoria and Adele are gonna have a fight!” Sam exclaimed with glee.

Honoria crossed her arms over her chest and glared at them when they reached the stairs. “We are *not* going to have a fight. She’s wearing my dress without permission and she’s going to have to give it back.”

“No fight?” Sam whined in disappointment.

“Could you at least shove her around some?” Thackary asked. “I’m mad at her.”

"Shove her around yourself," Honoria said, then let her arms fall to her sides. *Not* the best example she could have set. "Never mind. That's a bad idea."

"No, it's not," Thackary said, excitement in his voice. "I think it's a fine idea!"

She rolled her eyes, turned and continued up the staircase. "Adele!" she shouted down the hall.

Adele poked her head out of her room—and sure enough, she was wearing Honoria's pink dress. "Oh bugger!" she squealed, ducked back inside and slammed the door.

Honoria hurried down the hall and went to open it. Locked. "Adele! I need my dress!"

"Can't you wear your blue one?" came the muffled reply.

"No, Mother wants me to wear the pink one!" She wondered why she was even bothering.

"But I like the pink one!" Adele protested.

Honoria let her head fall against the door and groaned. "Fine, you wear it. Just don't ruin it." She stepped back and saw Thackary and Sam at the top of the staircase, watching with barely restrained glee. Unfortunately for them, no spilled blood was forthcoming. Fashion just wasn't worth fighting over. Maybe she wouldn't change at all and serve instead. Servants weren't supposed to look good, were they?

The door to Adele's room suddenly opened. She poked her head out. "If you really want to wear it, I'll take it off."

Honoria was far past caring. "Don't worry about it—just don't drag the hem and get it all dirty." Adele was a few inches shorter—ankle-length for Honoria was floor-length for her.

"Really? Thank you, Honoria! I hope Mother will make me one just like it. At least use the same fabric."

"It is pretty, isn't it?" Honoria said grudgingly.

"What are you going to wear then?" Adele asked.

She shrugged. "Doesn't really matter."

Adele stepped into the hall. "What's wrong? Don't Aunt Sadie and Uncle Harrison want you to dress up?"

"They do. I just don't feel like it." In fact, she felt like going back to bed and reading a book. She might've tried it if she wasn't hoping to convince her family to let her go abroad. Maybe she should clean up a little for that. "I'll find something to wear, don't worry." She turned to leave.

Adele grabbed her hand. "Thanks, cousin," she said, pulling her into a hug.

Honoria smiled. "You're welcome." She headed back down the hall, stuck her tongue out at Thackary and Sam in passing, then trotted down the stairs and went home. Yes, England would bring about a good change in her life. Look—she'd just stuck her tongue out at her cousins! What proper English lady would do such a thing? Maybe that was why Major was courting Miss Lynch. *She* didn't go racing across the prairie like a madwoman, now did she?

Perhaps she'd ask Maddie what it was like living at court, glean a few pointers on proper etiquette. That would show Father and Mother she was interested in what they termed "growing up"—and sell the idea of sending her across the Atlantic. She laughed to herself as she went back up to her room. She supposed her father would still put up a fuss and drive her crazy.

Well, if he was going to do so regardless, Honoria would just as soon be an ocean away.

Chapter Eleven

"Honoria Cooke!" Harrison and Sadie said at the same time as they watched their daughter come down the stairs. "Why aren't you wearing your pink dress?" her mother added.

"Adele is," Honoria said as she reached the bottom. "I'd forgotten I loaned it to her. It looks better on her anyway. Maybe I should let her keep it."

Her father looked her up and down. "And what are *you* wearing?" he asked sharply.

Honoria glanced at her simple blue calico day dress. "I just didn't see why we have to put on our Sunday best when this is perfectly fine."

"It is *not* perfectly fine," her mother said tersely. "March right back up to your room and change."

"There's no time," her father said as flipped open his pocket watch. "If Honoria wants to look sloppy tonight, then that's her business. She's not a child."

"Sloppy?" Honoria said, trying her best to look offended. "Thank you, Papa. You look nice too."

Her mother sighed and headed for the kitchen in frustration. Her father watched her go, then faced the door and straightened his jacket.

"Are they here already?" she asked.

"Not yet, but they will be any minute." He straightened his jacket again.

"Papa, why are you so nervous?"

He looked at her in shock, then quickly sobered. "I'm not nervous. I'm just…in a state of anticipation."

Uncle Colin burst through the front door. "Where are they?!"

Harrison about jumped out of his skin. "Great Scott, man, learn to knock!"

Uncle Colin slapped him on the back. "Startled you, eh, old chap?"

Honoria leaned against the banister. "You're *both* nervous."

Colin sighed. "Of course we are. It's been a long time since we've seen the Bergs."

"I dare say, an eternity," Honoria said. "Since yesterday."

"Honoria…" her father warned.

"That's not what I meant," Colin said. "Yes, we saw them yesterday, along with the rest of the town. But this is different."

"How is it different?" she asked as she followed them into the parlor.

Her father sat in one of the wing chairs and tapped his fingers on his knee. "She's right. We're both a little, shall we say, agitated?"

Honoria sat next to her uncle on the settee. "But why, Papa? I don't understand."

"In short, sweetling, people change," he said. "I guess your uncle and I are afraid that Andel and Maddie have changed after being away so long."

"Your father's quite right," Uncle Colin agreed. "Simply put, we just run a ranch. Your Uncle Duncan has an estate—a rather large one, mind you, but still only an estate. I can't imagine what running an entire *country* must be like."

"Did they seem different to you yesterday?" she asked.

Her uncle and father glanced at one another. "No, come to think of it, they didn't," her father said.

"Perhaps we are worrying over nothing," Uncle Colin suggested.

"I know the stories of how they became royalty," Honoria said. "You don't think it's gone to their heads, do you?"

"If yesterday was any indication, no," said her uncle. "He seemed perfectly normal. For Andel, that is."

"Quite right, brother. If anything, our wives are the ones to blame."

"Oh no," Honoria's mother said she entered the parlor with her aunt. "Don't drop this on us! There's nothing wrong with wanting to clean house and prepare a nice supper for guests."

"And forcing everyone to put on their Sunday best?" Honoria added with a smile.

"Not everyone, obviously." Her mother glared at her. "But you have to remember, Andel and Maddie have never met you children. Of course we want you all looking your best. So please go and find a nicer dress before—"

The sound of a wagon rolling into the barnyard interrupted her mother's statement. Her father jumped to his feet. "Good grief, they're here! All right, everyone, remain calm!"

Uncle Colin burst out laughing. "So much for not being nervous. I daresay, brother, if you don't calm down, you're going to do yourself a mischief."

"Egads!" her father muttered, wiping his hand over his face. "I don't know what's gotten into me."

"Well, it's been a long time since we've had guests in this house," her mother said.

"With the exception of the chap who brought Honoria home last month, after her little…accident," Uncle Colin put in.

Heat shot through Honoria at the mention of Major. *Oh, Uncle*, she thought to herself. *Did you have to bring him up?*

A knock sounded at the door. "I'll get it!" Uncle Colin said cheerfully and marched out of the parlor.

"Honoria, it's too late to change now," her mother said. "Run upstairs and fetch your brothers and sister."

"All right." She left the parlor and was halfway up the stairs before her uncle got a chance to open the door. She gathered her siblings together, shooed them down, then studied her reflection in a small mirror in her brother's room before following. She hadn't even bothered to fix her hair. "Oh well, what's one ragamuffin in the bunch?" she said aloud. "All the more reason to send me somewhere for finishing, I hope."

She knew this was an opportunity to pitch her idea—but she didn't feel much like company. Bed and a good sulk seemed much more attractive right now, but there was no help for it. She'd have to get through the evening whether she wanted to or not. With a sigh, she left her brothers' room, went down stairs and…

"Good evening Miss Cooke."

Honoria's eyes widened, and she almost choked.

Major Comfort looked around as her parents and the rest of the family greeted the Bergs. "What's the matter? Cat got your tongue?"

She audibly gulped and glanced at her cousin Adele, who looked lovely as ever in *her* pink dress. Her cousins must have come through the back door and into the parlor while the Bergs entered through the front. All beside the point now—what was Major doing here?

"Well?" he said.

"I… I…" Unable to think of what to say, she took the last few stairs—and tripped!

Thankfully, he grabbed her before she fell flat on her face. "Easy there…"

Honoria was now flush against him, his arms around her. Her breathing stopped as she stared up into those wonderful blue eyes of his.

"I'll say it again," he said quietly. "Good evening, Miss Cooke."

"Good evening," she managed. Barely.

"Honoria!" her father called from the parlor. Her eyes drifted in his direction even as his fixed on Major. *Uh-oh...* "Mr. Comfort! Take your hands off my daughter!"

Major managed to keep his bemused smile even as he set her upright and stepped away. "She was about to fall, sir."

"What are you doing here?" her father demanded as he reached the bottom of the stairs.

"I invited him," Mr. Berg said as he stepped into the foyer.

Her father glanced between the two men. "Whatever for?"

Now Honoria *really* wanted to go back upstairs and hide. If it had been any other man…

"Because his sister and her husband were invited," Mr. Berg explained.

"What?" her father said, confused. "Sadie!"

Honoria's mother joined them. "What's all the yelling about, dear?"

"Did you invite Eli and Pleasant Turner to supper?"

"Oh yes…good heavens, Harrison, I told you about that

earlier. I'd invited them several days ago, so when we knew the Bergs were coming this evening, there was no point in cancelling…"

"Besides," Mr. Berg added, "I wanted to hear more about Georgia and their plantation."

"Which we no longer have," Major said quietly. "I really don't understand your interest, sir."

"Parts of Dalrovia have a similar climate and soil to your coastal plain, so I wanted to learn more about growing cotton and the other crops in that part of the country."

"Are you thinking of growing some of them where you come from?" Major asked.

"Along with a few other ideas, if you've time to talk about them," Mr. Berg said with a smile.

"Of course, I'd be happy to."

Honoria barely heard their exchange. She stood and watched Major, fascinated at the way his left earlobe moved when he talked. When she caught herself leaning toward him, she took a quick step back for safety's sake. The feel of having his arms around her still lingered.

"Well, I think everyone's here," her mother said, peering out the open front door as she clasped her hands in front of her. "Eli and Pleasant just drove up." She looked at Mr. Berg. "Are you and Maddie ready to meet the children?"

Mr. Berg glanced at the crowd in the parlor. "Can everyone fit in here, or do we need to line them up outside?"

Sadie laughed. "That's not a bad idea, Andel. Maybe we should."

"Let's do it, then." The giant headed for the parlor, her mother on his heels. Her father had already been pulled back into the chaos.

But Major hadn't budged. "May I escort you outside?" he asked, offering her his arm.

She bit her lower lip, unsure of what to do. *He's just*

being a gentleman, she told herself. *And he's courting Miss Lynch.* She had no business even speaking to him—

"Honoria?"

Her head snapped up. "What did you call me?"

"That is your name, isn't it?"

"Yes, but…"

"Can you fault me if I wish to use it?"

"But Mr. Comfort…"

"After all we've been through?"

Friends called each other by their first name, didn't they? Perhaps that's what he was offering—friendship. Maybe it was his way of making up for his borderline-improper behavior when he'd brought her to town and home. She swallowed hard and looked at him. "Does this mean that I should call you Major?"

"Major is fine. Though my brothers call me Quince."

She had to swallow a giggle. Being named after a military rank was one thing, but after a fruit? Then again, he did look good enough to eat…*stop, stop,* stop, *Honoria!* she told herself. "I'll try Major, then," she finally said.

The chaos of the parlor had started to file out the door. The children were loud and excited, clamoring for position to see who could get outside first. Honoria's cousin Jefferson, two years her junior, brought up the rear, rolling his eyes at her as he motioned with his hands to speed his younger brothers along. The adults came next.

"Coming?" Major asked with a smile. "Though I hope we're not going to be tested to see if we remember all their names."

"You'll learn them in time," Honoria said. "That is, if you're around long enough."

Major offered his arm again. "I always did like a challenge."

She licked her bottom lip and, unable to help herself,

said, "Then I'll make sure I test you later." And together, they followed the rest of her family outside.

Archibald Lynch paced his hotel room like a caged animal. He'd been biding his time, allowing Lucretia the opportunity to work her feminine wiles on the Comfort men. *Any* of the Comfort men—he wasn't picky about which one at this point. But dash it all, what was taking her so long?

Ever since that luncheon in the Denver café, when he'd overheard Buford Comfort speaking with his sister-in-law (or some other relative, he still wasn't sure) about his precious plantation and how prosperous it was, he'd been determined his daughter would marry into it. Then he'd be taken care of as well.

So far, the Comforts had fallen for the story of their father sending Lucretia to be Major's mail-order bride. But that wasn't going to last—it was only a matter of time before one of them heard back from their father or Mrs. Pettigrew of the Pettigrew Mail-Order Bride Agency. Lucky for him, he'd overheard that part of Buford's conversation as well, how he wanted his sons to marry and was thinking of suggesting to the eldest that he order a bride.

Granted, things would've gone more smoothly had Buford actually gone through with it, but when Archibald and Lucretia went to see Mrs. Pettigrew, there were no applicants from any of the six Comfort boys. That was when Archibald decided to take a leap and create his own application and subsequent marriage contract.

He'd even gone so far as to get acquainted with Buford Comfort himself by following him around. The man talked of nothing but his beloved Comfort Fields to anyone who'd listen and that he was only visiting his sister-in-law for a time. From what Archibald could gather, poor Buford had suffered some sort of a shock and was convalescing in

Denver. Why anyone would want to convalesce there, he had no idea. The weather in Savannah was so much nicer this time of year.

All in all, his plan had moved along perfectly until they'd gotten to the benighted burg of Clear Creek. He was patient, a trait that made him a good con artist, but his money wasn't going to last forever. He'd have to get Lucretia married and soon, preferably to the eldest brother, who stood to inherit most of the plantation. He'd seen it before—fathers usually passed everything to the eldest son, or most of it anyway.

"Daddy, I thought Major was joining us for supper!" Lucretia whined.

"The blind man downstairs gave me a message from him. I'm afraid he was called away."

"What?" she said with a huff. "How rude! And I just had that Mrs. Mulligan mend my best dress! I can't think how it got torn! I wish I could have some new ones made, but this backwoods town doesn't even have a dressmaker! When are we going get out of here?"

"When you're married. Then we'll head to Georgia and your new home. Those Comfort boys can't possibly plan on staying here. I think they've come to sow their wild oats."

"And their father let them? Men!" She twisted a lock of hair around her finger. "Have you gotten Major to tell you any more about Comfort Fields?"

"No. He seems touchy about the subject—won't discuss Savannah or Georgia or any of it. But don't worry. If their father can afford to let his sons have an extended holiday out west, the family must be rich indeed."

"I've heard of men doing silly things before, but this is ridiculous! I hope he gets this out of his system before we marry!"

"He will, then he'll whisk you away to Comfort Fields."

"I can't wait to see it. Perhaps we could get married there?"

"And travel across the country with your betrothed? No, no, my dear. It's best to get married here in Clear Creek."

"If you say so," she pouted.

"Daddy knows best, dearest. Speaking of your betrothed, when do you think he'll ask you?"

She rolled her eyes and plopped herself into a chair. "How should I know? I'm not a mind reader. I thought sure he'd ask after lunch yesterday, but that beast of a man and his wife showed up and everyone went 'plumb loco' as the locals say."

"Yes, they certainly did. Come to think, I heard something yesterday but..." He shook his head.

"What?"

"It's nothing. I must've heard wrong." He went to her chair, bent and took her hand in his. "You just keep showing Mr. Comfort that pretty smile of yours and he'll come around. Soon, I hope."

"I wish he'd smile back," she commented dryly. "I noticed he smiled plenty when that country girl came in the mercantile."

"What girl?"

"That Cooke woman. Her family owns the big ranch outside of town. Horrible creature. Major hardly batted an eye at me once he saw her!"

"Really?" her father said. He rubbed his chin in thought and glanced at the door. Where had Major Comfort got to this evening? Was he with the Cooke woman? The last thing Lucretia needed was competition—sure, she was pretty enough, but she wasn't bright, couldn't cook and had the temperament of a rattler when annoyed. She'd been on her best behavior since coming to Clear Creek. But what if her best wasn't enough? "I'm afraid you'll have to step things up with Mr. Comfort, my dear. As you know, time is of the essence."

"You don't have to remind me," she sneered. "I'm doing the best I can! So, Daddy, what are you going to do about it?"

"Not to worry, my dear," he assured. "I'll make sure to...remove the competition."

Lucretia smiled. "Thank you, Daddy."

"Think nothing of it."

Chapter Twelve

Honoria wasn't sure how it happened—the chaos of the evening, an unconscious effort on her part or divine intervention—but somehow she found herself next to Major at the dining table. Her heart thundered in her chest and she hoped no one else noticed. She even stole a glance at her bosom to see if it was rising and falling with each heartbeat. She swore it did, several times, but when she looked, all was still. My heavens, but was the dining room unusually hot?

"Andel," her father said. "Would you like to say the blessing, for old time's sake?"

Mr. Berg smiled. "Certainly." He folded his hands in front of him, bowed his head and closed his eyes. "Thank you, Lord, for friendship, camaraderie, old acquaintances and new. We ask that you bless this food and everyone at this table. Amen."

"I think that's the longest supper prayer you've ever said, Andel," Uncle Colin said with a grin.

"At least no one wrote it for me," he joked.

Everyone stared at him in confusion until Maddie leaned forward and said, "Speeches."

"Speeches?" Aunt Belle said. "Do you give a lot of them?"

"Only when I have to. Maddie has to do most of them."

"You will have to explain to us how everything works in your country," Harrison said. "I'd be fascinated to know." He gave Honoria and Major a glance, then returned his attention to the Bergs. "But first, how long do you plan on staying in Clear Creek?"

"Actually," Mr. Berg said, "we are on holiday. We had some business in New York and Washington City, but now our time is our own."

"That's wonderful!" Sadie happily. "How long can you stay?"

"We plan to leave after Christmas," he said. "We wanted to spend the holiday among friends. It was a hard choice to make because of the children."

"Oh, that's right," said Belle. "Will they be disappointed you're not there?"

"My mother and Anton are with them," explained Maddie. "We'll join them for the new year."

"*After* the new year, she means," Mr. Berg said with a smile.

"Oh! Yes, of course," Maddie said in a rush. "After all, we couldn't possibly get home *that* fast, could we?"

Honoria studied them. Was that a warning glare Mr. Berg was giving his wife?

"What sort of climate does your country have?" Major asked.

"Very diverse—one of our ministers has compared it to California, with all the different regions," Mr. Berg explained. "We have all four seasons. That's part of why we're looking into planting alternative crops, to take full advantage."

"Such as cotton," Major offered.

"Exactly," Mr. Berg replied. "And I'd still like to speak with you about that. Perhaps tomorrow?"

"Of course, I'll make myself available. Would afternoon suit you?"

"Quite."

"Er...speaking of tomorrow," Harrison said as he reached for the mashed potatoes. "I hear that a party is being planned?"

"Party?" Colin said. "Oh yes, a *party*." He grinned at the Bergs at the other end of the table.

"Oh my," Maddie said. "I knew our visit would cause a stir, but I didn't think you'd throw us a party."

"We threw a huge party for Duncan and Cozette on their last visit," Sadie said. "Of course we'd throw one for you. Especially if you're going to be here for Christmas!"

"How old are your children?" Honoria asked.

Maddie took a piece of chicken off the platter her husband offered. "Our oldest, Asger, is thirteen. Raina, our daughter, turned eleven at the end of August. And Valentin—Vale, we call him—turned nine at the beginning of August."

"Two princes and a princess," Belle said with a smile.

The Bergs glanced at each other and nodded. "Another reason they're not with us," Maddie said. "For reasons of safety."

"What do you mean?" Major asked with a raised eyebrow. Honoria could see he was truly curious as to why, but she suspected she understood.

"One heir has to be kept safe at all times," Maddie said. "If something were to happen to us, Asger would ascend to the throne."

Major leaned back in his chair and stared at them. "If someone had told me I'd be sitting here having supper with a king and queen in Clear Creek, I never would've believed them."

"Prince consort," four people corrected, then laughed.

"I am not a king," Andel explained to Major. "I only married *into* the royal family, so 'prince consort' is my proper title. Among the crowned heads of Europe, they can be very particular about those titles."

"My apologies," Major replied. "And I can see why you bring with you your…escort."

"Is that what ya call 'em?" Eli asked. "'Cause I call them a pain in the—"

"Eli!" Pleasant warned, then sent the Bergs an apologetic look. "Sorry."

"Yes, the guard," Maddie said with a sigh. "And you're right, Mr. Turner—at times they can be a nuisance."

"Beggin' your pardon, Mrs. Berg, but I don't think I could stand it if'n a pack of men followed me and my wife around wherever we went," Eli said sympathetically.

Maddie smiled in understanding. "I'm sure they're enjoying Sadie's fried chicken."

"We could make room at the table for them," Colin suggested.

"The guard do not eat with us—they're here to protect us," Mr. Berg explained. "Myself, I'd rather travel with just Maddie, but…" He sighed heavily. "…we have the kingdom to think of. They need to assure we're safe and sound. So being accompanied by the Royal Guard goes with the job."

"As a former Captain of the Guard, you should know," Maddie teased.

Mr. Berg shrugged in resignation and took a bite of chicken. The rest of the evening was spent bringing Andel and Maddie up to date on events in Clear Creek over the last few years.

Honoria watched as Major listened in fascination. He was learning all about them, about her, without her uttering a word. She tried not to giggle when Major arched an eyebrow at the retelling of some prank she'd pulled on her siblings or vice-versa. He seemed to especially like hearing about Savannah's ingenuity when it came to practical jokes. "Your younger sister sounds like a force to be reckoned with," he whispered to her at one point. "She's going to be a firecracker when she gets older."

"Firecracker?" Honoria said with a laugh. "More like an artillery barrage. Father's already making jokes about the 'poor bloke' who marries her."

He laughed, drawing everyone's attention. "Sorry," he said then dabbed at his mouth with a napkin. "Miss Cooke has quite the sense of humor."

"'Miss Cooke' now, is it?" she mumbled out the corner of her mouth.

He looked at her and smiled. "Miss Cooke," he said, louder than he needed to. "Would you do me the honor of allowing me to call you by your first name?"

Harrison practically choked on his potatoes. "First name?! Now see here, there's no call for that."

"I beg to differ, sir," Major stated calmly. "After all Miss Cooke and I have been through, I believe it appropriate."

Harrison dropped his fork on his plate with a clatter. "Been through?"

"Hello, what's this?" Mr. Berg glanced between Harrison and Honoria.

Oh dear. She'd better think fast. "Er, ah… Mr. Comfort… came to my aid one day."

"Do tell?" Mr. Berg said with a smile.

"Gladly," Harrison said darkly. "My *darling* daughter challenged him to a horse race, lost and broke her ribs in the process!"

"Bruised, Papa," Honoria corrected. Was he really going to embarrass her like this in front of everyone? "I bruised my ribs."

"Bruised, broken, who cares? It never should've happened in the first place!"

Honoria wanted to slide under the table. "Papa, calm yourself."

"That accident was entirely preventable, young lady!"

"Harrison," Sadie interjected, "I don't think this is the right time..."

"Right time?! She could have been killed!"

"And Mr. Comfort came to her aid?" Mr. Berg asked.

Harrison opened and closed his mouth a few times, clearly flustered. "Well, he could hardly do otherwise—he was there! But that's beside the point!"

"The point, sir, is that your daughter is safe and sound now," Major said diplomatically. "No harm done, as they say."

"That's still no excuse to call her by her first name," Harrison grumbled.

Honoria knew she might regret this, but her dander was up. "I don't mind," she said, taking a biscuit.

Her father's eyes popped. "Honoria!"

"And I'll call you Major," she told him, ignoring her father.

"I'd like that," he whispered.

A thrill went up her spine as her father abruptly stood. "Sadie! Time for dessert!" He grabbed her mother by the arm, practically yanking her from her seat and dragging her from the room.

Colin snorted and also stood. "Perhaps we'd better go help them. What say you, Belle?"

She pressed her lips together to keep from laughing and winked at Honoria. "Oh, definitely yes."

"What's all the fuss about?" Eli asked.

"You've been too busy holding your wife's hand underneath the table," Mr. Berg said casually.

Eli and Pleasant's shoulders jerked as they pulled their hands apart. Honoria's snort of laughter rivaled Colin's.

"I don't see what the hubbub is about either," Pleasant said. "We had a lovely meal and conversation, and now this!"

"I do like the part where Honoria's about to get a lickin' from Pa," added Maxwell, who'd walked in from the kitchen where the children were eating.

"Thank you, Max," Honoria said sarcastically.

"You're welcome."

"Harrison has always been overprotective," Mr. Berg told Honoria. "Even when your mother was carrying you."

"The whole town remembers," Honoria groaned. "They never let me forget it."

Maddie laughed. "He *was* horrible, wasn't he? But..." Her voice dropped to a hiss. "...when I was carrying Asger, Andel was just as bad if not worse."

"I was not," he replied, calmly but firmly.

"You had a dozen guards follow me everywhere I went," she stated flatly.

"*Eight* guards, not a dozen. And that was a demand of the privy council, which *you* acceded to..."

"After your impassioned plea to the council about the 'current fragility of the royal line'..."

Major laughed. "See, things could be worse. What if your father had guards at his disposal?"

Honoria paled and unconsciously leaned toward him. "Perish the thought."

Mr. Berg made a show of clearing his throat. "What kind of pie did you bake, Honoria?"

"Pumpkin," she said with a smile, her eyes never once leaving Major's.

Mr. Berg took note and gave Major a pointed look. "Do you like pumpkin pie, Mr. Comfort?"

Major didn't notice—*his* eyes were on Honoria. "It's a favorite."

"Fancy that," Mr. Berg said. "You'll get to try some of Honoria's cooking. Though perhaps you already have," he added archly.

Maddie slapped him on the arm. "Andel!"

"I made the potatoes," she volunteered dreamily.

"They were excellent," Major replied.

"Dear Lord," Maxwell groaned, rolling his eyes.

Eli began to chuckle.

"What are you laughing at?" Pleasant asked. "My brother loves mashed potatoes."

"Trust me, dear—taters are the *last* thing on his mind."

Now Maddie rolled her eyes. "Mr. Comfort? Why don't you take Honoria out onto the front porch? I'm sure after all the commotion of the evening you'd like some peace and quiet."

Major slowly turned at her, still smiling vacantly. "Don't mind if I do." He stood. "Shall we?"

Honoria could only stare.

"And I think *we* should go help out in the kitchen," Maddie told the other adults.

"Won't that look suspicious?" Andel asked.

"Only if they're up to something." She leaned toward Major. "Are you?"

"Oh, I'm sure the thought never crossed my mind." Major winked at Honoria and offered her his arm. "Shall we?"

A blush rising up her neck, Honoria stood and wrapped her arm through his.

Soon, Eli and Pleasant were all alone in the dining room. "Tarnation, I thought they'd never leave." Eli leaned toward his wife for a kiss.

Pleasant pulled away. "Eli Turner! How can you sit here and want to spark with me when my brother and Honoria are out there on the front porch? Don't you want to know what's going on?"

Eli's brow furrowed. "Why? I'm more concerned with what's right in front of me." He pulled her close and kissed her soundly.

"I declare!" she exclaimed when he finally broke it. "But aren't you the least bit curious?"

"Nope—that's Harrison's job. He's worse than any deputy, that's for sure." He leaned toward her again.

"Merciful heavens." She pushed him away. "Wait until we get home. Besides, someone's got to chaperone." She stood.

Eli reluctantly nodded. "Yeah, given what I just saw. But what about him courtin' that gal staying at the hotel with her daddy?"

"Oh fiddle-dee-dee! Major isn't interested in her. He's just trying to figure out who she can marry here instead of traveling all the way back to wherever she came from. He's like that, you know—tries to take care of everybody. But with Honoria…well, I haven't seen him look that interested in a gal in…actually, I've *never* seen him like this."

"Well, I'll be." He got up. "We better hurry!"

She put a hand on her hip. "Oh, *now* you're interested?"

"He deserves to be warned."

"Warned? About what?"

"About Honoria. She's got her own way of thinkin' and doin'. We'd better make sure yer brother can handle her."

"Eli Turner, you make her sound horrible."

"She ain't horrible, but she does speak her mind."

"My brother faced off against Sherman's Army of the Tennessee and survived—he is perfectly capable of handling Honoria Cooke!" Pleasant folded her arms in front of her. "And he can speak his mind too, rest assured." She took her husband's hand and headed for the parlor.

Once there, they sat on the settee facing the window. They did their best to look innocent as Harrison and Sadie came in carrying trays of dessert and coffee. "Has everyone left the dining room?" Harrison asked, glancing around.

"I thought everyone went to the kitchen with you," Eli replied. "'Cept Honoria and Major."

Harrison's eyes bulged like a bullfrog's. "What? Where are they?"

"Calm down, Harrison—they're just out on the porch. And nothin's happened that shouldn't—Pleasant and me are sittin' right here keepin' an eye on 'em. Major ain't about try somethin' untoward when his sister's sittin' on the other side of the winder."

"And if his sister wasn't sitting there?" Harrison huffed and set the tray of desserts down.

Sadie seemed to be losing patience. "But she is, Harrison."

Undeterred, he headed straight for the window, ignoring Andel entering the parlor. Then he suddenly stopped, turned and went toward the front door instead.

Andel Berg reached out a long arm and grabbed Harrison by the shoulder, stopping him dead. "What kind of pie is this?"

"Let go of me! I need to get out there."

"And do what—pour them coffee?" Andel managed to sound threatening as he asked it.

"I'll take care of that," Colin interjected, snatching two plates off the dessert tray. "Belle, could you bring the coffee?"

"Of course, dear!" Belle made no effort to hide her smirk as she grabbed two cups and saucers and sidled past as Mr. Berg pinned Harrison where he stood. Voices were heard on the porch as the front door opened and closed, then the muffled sounds of Colin and Belle serving Major and Honoria dessert. Within a minute the older couple had returned. "All sorted," Colin declared, rubbing his hands together. "Now, what shall I have—apple or pumpkin?"

"You gave Mr. Comfort the pumpkin pie Honoria made?" Mr. Berg asked.

"Of course." Colin took for himself a piece of apple pie and a cup of coffee and sat in a wing chair.

"Perhaps the rest of us should go back into the dining room," Sadie suggested. "As soon as the children are finished with their dessert they'll want to hear stories, and Jefferson and Edith are already getting tired…"

"Sounds like a splendid idea." Andel released Harrison, took two plates and headed for the dining room. Maddie grabbed a couple of cups of coffee and followed.

"We'll stay in the parlor," Eli volunteered, handing Pleasant a piece of pumpkin pie.

"Then for Heaven's sake, man, open the window!" Harrison blurted.

"Too chilly for that," Eli demurred.

Harrison pointed at the window. "I want to know what's going on out there!"

Sadie put her foot down. "Harrison Cooke, do I have to hogtie you to get you to calm down? As much as *I'd* like to know what's going on out there, Honoria deserves some privacy. Besides, Andel's guards are outside, doing… whatever it is they do."

"That's right, old chap," Colin said around a mouthful of pie. "You can't get better chaperones than two squads of royal guardsmen."

"They're *not* courting!" Harrison stated sternly. "And there are four guards out there, not two squads!"

"Sure they're not courting," Sadie muttered.

"Mr. Cooke, you have nothing to worry about," Pleasant insisted. "I know my brother, and he would never be more than a perfect gentleman around a lady."

Harrison saw he was objecting alone. "Very well. But if anything happens, I'm going to shoot him."

"Harrison, that's enough!" Sadie grabbed his arm and started to drag him toward the dining room, where the Bergs were laughing at the scene.

"I find nothing funny about this, Andel!" Harrison raged. "Just wait until your daughter is old enough!"

Andel wiped a tear from his eye. "Raina is already promised to young Lord Stefan, heir to the throne of the Duchy of Vodina. Nice boy, likes to paint. I've no such worries as you."

Harrison turned to Sadie. "I want a monarchy."

She rubbed her temples. "Lord, give me patience."

Harrison suddenly smiled. "Wait a moment… I thought Mr. Comfort was courting that Miss Lynch from town."

"We've determined that he ain't," Eli called from the parlor.

"Except perhaps in her own mind," Pleasant added.

But Harrison was pacing now, his brow furrowed. "Andel, I need a favor."

Sadie blanched as Colin and Belle entered the dining room and seated themselves at the table. "Oh no," Sadie said. "This can't be good."

"Judging from the look on my brother's face," Colin said, "I can guarantee it isn't."

Harrison grinned like the devil. "Oh, trust me—this is going to be splendid."

Chapter Thirteen

"So what were they like?" Zachary Comfort asked. He and Major had just returned to the men's camp after escorting Eli and Pleasant back to town from the Triple-C, and the six Comfort brothers were seated at the long dining table at one end of the camp's main cabin. The only other furniture in the room were several chairs and a beat-up sofa at the other end near the fireplace, a small bookcase and a hutch near the cook stove.

"What were who like, exactly?" Major asked.

"Come now, Quince," Darcy said. "The Bergs. I want to know why everyone in town is making such a fuss over them. That nonsense about royalty can't possibly be true."

"On the contrary, it's quite true. Dalrovia is a small country, but it does exist. Mrs. Berg is their queen, and Mr. Berg her consort. It's not that hard to believe once you know the story behind it."

"But what are they doing here right *now*?" Matt, the youngest, asked. "Why leave a palace?"

"I know they mentioned visiting Washington City, so perhaps they had dealings with the government. Besides, some of those old European palaces are in sorry condition, or so I've heard. For all we know, theirs is no better off than our old mansion at Comfort Fields."

His brothers displayed various reactions at the mention of the plantation home they no longer had, none of them positive. Finally Darcy waved it all off. "It would be interesting to talk with them."

Michael sighed. "Enough about them. Major, tell us why you *really* went to the Triple-C."

Major felt his chest tighten at the thought of Honoria. She'd looked beautiful, even though it was obvious she'd avoided dressing for the occasion. She was the type of woman that did what she wanted and the Devil take the hindmost. Sometimes he wanted to throttle her for her stubbornness, but it was also a huge part of her appeal. She was different than other women, and he liked the difference. She was as beautiful, wild and free as the rolling prairie surrounding Clear Creek.

"Quince?" Zachary waved a hand in front of his face. "You must have had some visit."

"Are you going to ask her to marry you?" Benedict, quiet until now, asked and glanced at the others. "It's bound to happen to one of us soon. And you are the oldest."

"Isn't that why Father ordered a bride for you?" Michael pressed.

"Except that Quince isn't interested in Miss Lynch," Benedict added with a grin.

Major was about to comment when Jasper Kiggins entered the cabin. "Gettin' mighty nippy out," he commented as he wiped his boots. "Wouldn't be 'sprised if it gets cold enough to snow soon. Long overdue..." He looked at the Comforts seated around the table. "I interrupt somethin'?"

Zachary laughed. "No, Jasper. We were just talking about women and marriage."

Jasper took off his coat and hung it on a peg near the

door. "Marriage…now there's a happy topic. Sure like to find me a wife someday."

"Isn't that why you're going to Oregon City come spring?" Benedict asked.

"Nope—Astoria. I'da left sooner, but I thought I'd better save up more money. 'Sides, it'll be easier to find a place in the spring. Oregon City's 'bout played out now, but Astoria's a fast-growin' town, and the ships comin' in all the time—should be plenty of women to choose from."

"I don't believe I've seen a man as eager as you to marry, Mr. Kiggins," Major said with a smile. "I'm sure I speak for all of us when I say I hope you find what you're looking for."

"I tell ya what, gents—I'll be thirty-five next month. Purty soon I'll be past my prime. If I wanna family, I better get a move on."

The men laughed as Jasper took a seat at the table. He had a scraggly beard and was missing a couple of teeth, but his dark eyes were full of kindness, and he was honest and a hard worker. The Comfort brothers would miss his company come spring.

"And," Jasper added, pointing at Major, "I might say the same for ya—ya ain't getting' any younger. Yer what—twenty-eight, twenty-nine?"

"Thirty in April," Major agreed reluctantly.

"There ya are. A tree gotta start producin' fruit 'fore the sap dries up, knowhatImean?"

"How come you never found a wife here?" Matt asked, taking the heat off his eldest brother.

Jasper snorted. "Shoot, everyone knows there's no women 'round here to marry."

The Comfort brothers glanced at one another. "Certainly there is," Michael said. "Honoria Cooke is of age to marry."

Major's gut twisted as jealousy shot through him like fire. It was all he could do not to glare at his brother for even mentioning Honoria was available. *Oh, get a grip*, he thought to himself.

"Honoria Cooke?!" Jasper scoffed. "Aw, no—I ain't loco! I wouldn't go within a mile of that girl if'n I know what's good for me."

"Why is that?" Matt asked, glancing at Major. "Our brother just had supper with her and her family."

Jasper's jaw dropped, and he studied Major as if inspecting him for damage. "Ya did what?"

Major shrugged. "I had supper at the Triple-C, yes." He studied Jasper in return, his brow furrowing. "From the look on your face, Mr. Kiggins, I gather you're surprised to see me here in one piece."

"Ya got that right," Jasper said. "Folks 'round here know Harrison Cooke'd soon as shoot a fella in the kneecap as let him get near his daughter."

"I sat next to her at supper," Major added, arching one eyebrow. "And he wasn't that bad—a little overprotective, but what father isn't?"

Jasper looked him over again. "Well, ya don't look any worse for wear. Harrison musta let ya off easy. But I bet I know why—it's on account of ya courtin' that Miss Lynch."

"Excuse me, sir, but I am in no wise courting Miss Lynch," Major objected.

"What?" Jasper asked. "But it's all over town the two of ya are gettin' hitched."

Major rolled his eyes and sighed. "Only because Miss Lynch is spreading it 'all over town'."

"Then what *are* you doing, Quince?" Michael asked in all seriousness. "You've been spending more time with her than with Miss Cooke."

"I've been stalling, if you must know—waiting to hear back from Father. I don't understand why he hasn't written."

"Why don't you write the bridal agency?" Matt suggested.

"I did, last week—but I haven't heard from Mrs. Pettigrew either. Before I send Miss Lynch on her way, I want all the facts. If she and her father decide to settle here… then I need to make things right. I think that's only fair."

"Of course," agreed Zachary. "But have you informed Miss Lynch?"

"On numerous occasions. But she doesn't seem to want to listen—she came here to get married, and is determined to do so." He looked around at his brothers. "I don't suppose any of you might be interested?"

"She isn't hard on the eyes…" Jasper said, more to himself than anyone else.

"She is on the ears," Benedict added dourly.

Darcy spoke for the others. "None of us are in any position to take care of a wife at present. Including you, Major."

"One more reason I cannot marry Miss Lynch," Major agreed. But then, it also meant he was in a pinch if he wanted to court Honoria! Great Scott, how had he not seen that? He didn't own any land, had no steady job, no money in the bank—and he couldn't rely on his father or brothers, as they were in the same position. Jasper Kiggins was way ahead of them on that score—and it had taken him five years to save up enough money for his planned move to Astoria.

He'd been so blinded by his attraction to Honoria that he hadn't thought about how he could possibly feed, clothe or shelter her. He had no way to even attempt it.

Jasper, oblivious to Major's sudden distress, glanced around the table. "Look on the bright side, fellas. If Miss

Lynch and her pa do settle here, ya'll have plenty of time to save up."

One by one, the brothers gave Jasper their attention. "I guess that makes me the lucky one," Matt said. "Being as I'm the youngest."

"Indeed it does," Michael agreed. "You'll have longer to save than any of us."

"Then that makes me lucky too, as I don't plan to marry anytime soon," Benedict added. He looked at Major. "Our daddy, on the other hand, thinks *you* ought to marry now."

Major sighed. "I still can't figure out why he took such a drastic step."

"Because he's a desperate man, Quince," Darcy pointed out. "He has been, ever since we lost the plantation." Other heads around the table nodded.

"Gentlemen?" Major said. "Can we find something to talk about other than women?"

Jasper chuckled. "Heck, 'round here that's about *all* we talk about." His eyes darted to the cabin's front door. "Speakin' of, where is everybody else?"

"They're still in town," Zachary said. "When we were there, I noticed the others' horses in front of the saloon."

"It's a good thing we ain't far from Clear Creek," Jasper commented. "Pretty hard to ride home in the dark after a few drinks."

"That it is," Benedict agreed.

But Major had gone silent. What did he have right now, other than courtly manners? The fact began to pound at him, obliterating any thoughts of courting Honoria. Even if her father came to like him personally, he would certainly oppose a match on the grounds that he had no resources to provide for a wife.

No matter how much he liked Honoria—and, he was

discovering, he more than liked her—he had absolutely nothing to offer her as a husband.

Honoria lay in the soft green grass, a gentle breeze tickling her nose and lifting wisps of her hair.

A large hand reached over and brushed the wisps aside. She turned her head, feeling the pillow of meadow softness beneath it, and looked up into the piercing blue of Major's eyes. He was lying on his side next to her, his upper body propped up on one elbow, his head held by his hand. She studied every beautiful inch of him. He was magnificent.

Ever so slowly he leaned over her, bringing his lips within a hair's breadth of hers. "I love you, Honoria," he whispered against her mouth. "I'll love you until the day I die."

Honoria's breathing quickened. Her heart thundered in her chest at the closeness and she thought she might faint. Unable to help herself, she reached up, tangled her fingers in his hair and closed the distance between them…

"Honoria! Are you still in bed? Get up and get dressed! Those chickens aren't going to feed themselves!"

Honoria's eyes popped open as she gasped. Good heavens, had she been panting? She quickly glanced around the room, hoping her mother hadn't seen her slumbering acts of *amour.* She sat up, her breathing ragged now, and felt the first deep pangs of loneliness. Emptiness. "No," she whispered and ran her fingers over her lips. She swore she could still feel Major's, even if it was just a dream.

She fell back against the pillows and stared at the ceiling as the first tear fell. "Oh noooo," she groaned aloud as reality sank in. She was *dreaming* about him! She must be more attracted to him than she thought. He was, after all, *very* handsome. And those eyes…oh heavens, those eyes…

She raised a hand and studied her fingers, fingers that

moments ago had clutched Major Comfort's hair in a dream and pulled his lips to hers. The memory of it made her feel almost wicked. Almost. Because as she thought on it, their kiss was anything but. It was like tasting a slice of heaven, where she felt so cherished and loved.

Why? Why had it been nothing but a dream?

More tears. She'd never felt like this before and didn't know what to do. Why did it have to hurt so much? "I don't understand," she whimpered.

"Honoria?" her mother yelled from down the hall. "Will you get up?"

"I'm coming!" she shouted back. She closed her eyes a moment and took a shaky breath. How could one dream affect her so? So what if she kissed him? But then, why was it so wonderful? Why did it feel so…right?

With a weary sigh she sat up, tossed back her blankets and stood. For some reason, she felt completely out of place. "What is wrong with me?" A shiver ran up her spine, and she rubbed her arms with her hands to chase it away.

"Honoria?!"

"I'm dressing!" she shouted back. She went to the window and looked outside. She'd lived at the Triple-C all of her life, yet she suddenly felt like she didn't belong there. Another wave of loneliness hit, and she shut her eyes against the tears threatening to escape. The last thing she needed was her mother asking questions about why she'd been crying. What could she tell her? *I had a dream about Major Comfort last night, he kissed me, but because of Father and Lucretia Lynch I can never have him, so either lock me in my room for the rest of my life or…*

Or…she did have another option, didn't she? She'd even been working toward it yesterday, before Major's arrival switched her onto another track entirely. But there was no reason she couldn't get back to pursuing it, and avoid her heart breaking even more severely.

Honoria decided she would keep the dream to herself—it was too private, too precious. And she would renew her plan to convince her parents she should leave Clear Creek and go to England.

"Are you all right?"

Major turned to find Michael standing in the wide-open door of the barn. He turned back to his horse and tightened the cinch of the saddle. "I…didn't sleep well last night."

"Nor did I. I don't think any of us did."

Major stopped what he was doing and looked at him. "Why is that?"

"I think after last night, we all went to bed realizing that we have a long road ahead of us."

Major nodded solemnly. "That we do."

"What are you going to do about Miss Lynch if you don't hear from Father? You don't even have the money to send her back."

"No, I don't." He stared at the saddle. "But that doesn't mean I'm going to marry her. I can't."

"Word around town is you can."

"You know as well as I do that Miss Lynch is the one spreading those rumors. I have no intention of marrying her and I've made myself clear on that score."

"Are you sure? Because then why would she say anything contrary?"

"I told her…" His face fell. What *had* he told her? He'd been so caught up with thinking about Honoria Cooke that he couldn't remember. Well, he did remember part of it. "I told her I was waiting to hear from Father to get this whole mess straightened out."

"So in other words, you didn't actually say no."

Major closed his eyes a moment, feeling a headache coming on. "Oh dear..."

Michael put his hands on his hips. "Quince, you always were the generous sort, always the one trying to take care of everybody else. I remember how that used to get you into trouble."

"And it still does. I'd better explain to Miss Lynch and her father in no uncertain terms that I am not going to marry her. And go into the reasons why."

"The sooner the better. They'll no doubt be angry, but they'll get past it." He sighed and raised his eyes to the ceiling. "It's odd to me that a Yankee would want his daughter married to one of us." He gave Major a bemused smile. "Even if she was raised in the South."

"Northerners in general don't resent us as much as many of us do them—part of the benefit of winning the war. But..." Major made a face. "She may have been raised in the South, but every time I ask the two about the difference in their accents, they become very evasive."

"Does she speak of her mother?"

"Only that she died when she was young." Major shook his head. "It doesn't really matter, does it? I'm not marrying her regardless."

"Nor am I."

"Nor are any of us—none of us can support anyone else right now." Major finished cinching up his saddle, then removed the stirrup off the saddle horn and put it back in place. "I feel sorry for her, coming all this way for nothing, not even the reward of a husband to hang on to. That's why I didn't outright tell her, even if she doesn't seem the type to faint."

"Except on purpose," Michael quipped. "But she's not your responsibility—she's Father's. He's the one that sent the poor thing out here."

"Maybe that's why I haven't heard back from him yet. He feels guilty."

"When did you send that letter?"

"Weeks ago. In fact, Mr. Lynch was as upset as I was and sent word to Mrs. Pettigrew at the same time. I remember because he took both our letters to the mercantile to post them with Wilfred."

"These things do take time, I suppose. I'm sure we'll be hearing from Father soon. Not to mention Mrs. Pettigrew."

Major grabbed the reins of his horse and started to lead it out of the barn. "I'm going to town."

"Whatever for?"

He mounted. "For the same reason any of us go to town, dear brother. To find some work." He gave his horse a little kick and was off. With any luck, he'd find them all some.

Chapter Fourteen

By the time Major arrived in town, it was mid-morning and the residents of Clear Creek were going about their business. Mr. Mulligan stopped sweeping the boardwalk in front of his saloon and waved at him. A couple of doors down, Levi Stone came out of the bank, stretched and gave him a nod in greeting. Major tipped his hat in return. Sheriff Turner was sitting in a chair in front of the sheriff's office speaking with Deputy Brandon O'Hare as he leaned against a post. Both of them smiled and waved as Major rode past.

He brought his horse to a stop, twisted in the saddle and looked behind him. The sheriff and his deputy had gone back to their conversation, Mr. Mulligan was still sweeping and Levi was heading into the bank. Other townsfolk passed, waved, smiled. The people here were friendly and kind. He and his brothers liked the town and its residents even if some of them were a little odd. Thoughts of Irene Dunnigan and her hatchet made him shiver, and he gave his horse a little kick to get him moving.

His heart stopped when he spied the Triple-C's wagon parked in front of Dunnigan's Mercantile. He stared at it, dumbstruck, then quickly scanned his surroundings for any sign of Honoria. But there was none. "You fool, stop it," he scolded himself. He steered his horse to a hitching post near the mercantile and dismounted. Once he'd tethered the animal, he went to the porch steps and took them two at a time. No reason, he just felt like it.

The bell over the door rang as he entered and he immediately locked eyes with Andel Berg. "Good morning."

Andel smiled. "Good morning, Mr. Comfort. Just the man I'd like to see."

"Oh?" Then he remembered their conversation from the night before. "Yes, of course—you wished to talk crops."

Andel walked over to him. "I find myself wanting to speak with you on a number of different matters. How much time do you have today?"

"That depends on when you'd like to talk."

"Now, if you're able."

Major glanced at Wilfred behind the counter. "Has anyone posted anything for the men's camp?"

"Sorry, Major," Wilfred said. "Nothing today—not yet, anyway. Maybe check back later this afternoon."

Major nodded and turned back to Andel. "It looks like I have all the time you require, sir."

"Excellent. I gather you are looking for work?"

"Always. You lived here once—you know how the men's camp works."

"That I do—I helped set it up. Though it was Cyrus Van Cleet's idea; I only assisted."

Major nodded and sighed.

"Is something the matter?" Andel asked.

"I...just have things on my mind."

Andel cocked his head to one side and grinned. "Did you hear that, Wilfred?" he said over his shoulder. "Mr. Comfort here looks like a man with woman trouble. Don't you think so?"

"Think so?" Wilfred chuckled. "I know so!"

"Well, then," Andel said with a happy smile. "That settles it!"

"Settles…what?" Major asked nervously. Were the rumors around town that bad?

Mr. Berg wrapped a long arm around Major's shoulders and yanked him against his huge frame. "It's definitely time for us to have our chat. About more than just agriculture."

Major had a very strong feeling this meeting wasn't going to bode well.

"Go easy on him, Andel," Wilfred said. "After all, he's not from around here."

"Then I think it's about time he became one of us, don't you?"

Wilfred chuckled. "Maybe so, but wait until this evening." He gave Andel a conspiratorial wink. "Less witnesses."

"Witnesses?" Major said. Was now a good time to panic?

"I quite agree, Wilfred," Andel chortled and pulled Major toward the door. "We'll take care of our other business first, then see to the more important matter."

"What matter would that be?" Major said, still trying to take in a proper lungful of air. He contemplated digging his heels in and refusing to go, but knew it wouldn't work—the giant outweighed him by eighty pounds or more.

"You'll see," Andel said cheerily as he opened the door and shoved Major through it.

"Hello there."

Honoria turned to find Mr. Lynch picking at his jacket. He plucked something off and flicked it away. "Good afternoon."

"Miss Cooke, is it?" he asked, smiling widely.

"Yes. And you're Mr. Lynch."

"Quite so. You haven't happened to have seen Lucretia, have you?"

"Misplaced her?" It slipped out before she had time to stop herself. She cringed and waited for his reaction.

"Yes, as a matter of fact. That or she's misplaced herself. She has a horrible sense of direction. I won't sleep at night until she's married."

Honoria felt something within her sink at his words. "Married." The word came out flat as a flapjack.

"Of course. In fact, I need to find her so we can see the preacher about a wedding date."

Honoria swallowed hard. "I see. Has Maj... Mr. Comfort asked her, then?"

"Everyone knows they're going to marry, my dear," he said with a chuckle. "Now I'd better be off. This day is wasting away." He took a few steps down the boardwalk and turned. "Oh, by the way, this town wouldn't happen to have a dressmaker I haven't been able to uncover yet, would it?"

"I'm afraid there's none to uncover," she said, her heart in her shoes. "We do have a ladies' sewing circle."

"A sewing circle? How quaint. But no matter—I'm sure Lucretia and Major will want to get married right away once I get things settled for them. My daughter has some lovely frocks she brought with her—she won't mind wearing one of those."

"A mail-order bride who didn't bring a wedding dress?" Honoria stated more than asked.

"Not all mail-order brides do," he said. "But someone like you, on the other hand..." He closed the distance between them. "Having been raised here, you probably have a wedding gown all ready, being of marriageable age and all."

"No, sir."

"No?" he said in feigned shock, a hand to his chest for emphasis. What was that about? "Well, I *am* sorry. It must be devastating to realize that spinsterhood awaits you."

"Excuse me?"

"Though I can't understand why a woman like you would make such a choice for herself, unless she knows she *can't* marry."

"Mr. Lynch, what are you talking about?"

"After all," he said with a chuckle, "look at all the eligible young men currently in town, and you not married to a one of them."

"I don't see that that is any of your business, sir..."

"What a pity. You're not such a bad-looking girl." His eyes wandered over her again, but the look in them had changed. He swallowed, sucked in a breath and straightened his jacket. "I'd best be on my way, Miss Cooke. Until we meet again?" With a tip of his hat he spun on his heel and walked off.

Honoria stared after him, still trying to make sense of the odd conversation. She felt strangely...deflated. No, insulted. She shook as if to rid herself of any spoor he'd left behind and continued on her way. To where, she didn't know.

She'd just come from visiting with Grandma Waller while her Uncle Colin took care of some business for the Dunnigans. Their wagon needed tending, and he'd offered to take it to the livery stable to have Chase Adams look at it. But Grandma had chores to take care of and sent her on her way. She now found herself at loose ends—which had led to that strange conversation with Mr. Lynch.

Now that that was over (thank Heaven for small favors!), she needed to find something else of interest. The mercantile was out—they wouldn't get anything new in until tomorrow at the earliest. She decided to walk down to the hotel and see if the Brodys wanted to have a cup of tea with her. But as she passed the saloon, she thought she heard a familiar Southern drawl. She stopped on the other side of the saloon doors, alert, ears straining to hear the voice again.

Nothing. She closed her eyes as her shoulders slumped. She swore she'd heard Major's voice, but apparently not. Besides, what would he be doing in the saloon at this time of day? She stood straight, squared her shoulders and continued toward the hotel.

Once there, Honoria went inside to find Aideen, Lorcan and Ada Brody's little girl, sitting in the middle of the lobby with her doll. She was a beautiful child, with her father's dark hair and, according to Lorcan, his mother's violet eyes. She looked up, saw Honoria and squealed in delight. "Do you want to play with me?" she asked, holding up her doll and wiggling it. "This is Mrs. Quirk!"

Honoria gathered her skirt and sat Indian-style next to her. "But you only have the one doll. What do I play with?"

Aideen thought for a second. "I can run upstairs and get you one."

"If you'd like. Is your mother upstairs?"

Aideen pointed at the dining room doors. "She's helping Mrs. Upton."

"Why don't you run upstairs and get your doll and I'll go speak with your mother?" Honoria suggested.

Aideen jumped to her feet. "All right. I'll bring down my puppy—you can play with him."

"Puppy? Did your parents get you a dog?"

Aideen pouted. "He's not a real puppy. He's a toy." She suddenly smiled. "But I pretend he's real."

"Can I play too?"

Honoria froze. She hadn't even heard Major come

through the doors! Then again, maybe he had already been in the hotel.

He walked around to stand in front of them. "Hello." He put his hands on his knees and bent down to get eye level with the child.

"*You* want to play?" Aideen asked in disbelief.

"You said you have a puppy. I love puppies," he said tenderly.

Aideen's face fell. "It's not a real puppy, sir."

He cocked his head. "Don't sound so disappointed. We can pretend it's real, right?"

The child's eyes brightened. "I'll run and get him right now!" She was off like a shot, racing up the staircase as fast as her little legs could carry her.

Major unexpectedly joined Honoria on the floor, and she laughed at the sight. "What are you doing?" she asked in shock.

"Sitting, if I may. Do you mind?"

Her spirits lifted. "Not at all. So long as you don't mind being made fun of if someone walks in on us. We wouldn't look so awkward if Aideen was still here."

"Then it will be fun to make folks wonder, won't it? 'Why ever *are* those two sitting on the floor?' they'll ask themselves."

"'They must have gone completely round the bend'," Honoria said with an amused smile.

"'Don't talk to Honoria and Major'," he quipped. "'They're not themselves today. They'll plop down wherever it suits them'."

Honoria laughed again, louder this time. There was a freedom in it, and she liked the feeling.

"You're so unlike other women," Major said, his voice serious now. "I can honestly say that I've never met anyone like you."

Honoria studied him. He stared at her with an appreciation she hadn't seen before. She felt herself blush. "Life would be rather boring if women were all the same. At least as far as men are concerned."

"What about you? How exciting would it be if all men looked alike, talked alike, acted alike? You'd be bored out of your minds."

"Yes, I daresay we would be." She watched him watch her. She liked it. That is, until her strange meeting with Mr. Lynch popped into her head. She drew her knees up, arranging her skirt and wrapping her arms around her legs. "What, um, brings you to town?"

"I came to check the board at the mercantile for job postings for the men's camp. Then I had a meeting with Mr. Berg."

"Oh yes, he wants to plant cotton in Dalrovia."

"Not cotton specifically, though the climate may be right for it in a few spots. But he does want to experiment with new crops for his people. I admire him for that."

"He's their ruler," she said. "It's his job to look after their welfare."

"And here my brothers and I thought looking after a wife would be a big job. This man has to care for an entire country."

The word "wife" got her attention. "Are you looking forward to caring for a wife, Mr. Comfort?"

He arched an eyebrow at her tone. "Eventually."

Jealousy pricked her, flushing out her anger. "Sounds like you haven't long to wait."

Stunned, he was about to comment when Aideen came running down the stairs, Miss Lynch on her tail. "Give me back my comb, you wretched little beast!" He and Honoria watched the girl hurry in their direction, her stuffed puppy in one hand, a silver comb in the other. She ran straight for them and collapsed on the floor. "I'm back!"

Miss Lynch was still bearing down on her. "I said, give me back my comb!"

Aideen looked up at her. "This is my mama's comb," she insisted.

"It most certainly is not, you little wretch!" Miss Lynch suddenly straightened, her eyes riveted on Major. "I mean… I need to see it," she said more calmly. "To make sure." She swallowed hard and clasped her hands in front of her. "Hello, Major."

He looked at Honoria before glancing up at her. "Yes?"

Miss Lynch's eyes went wide. "What are you doing sitting in the middle of the floor?"

"Waiting for Aideen," he stated simply.

"For a *child*? Whatever for?"

"Because he's going to play with me!" Aideen said gleefully, waving her puppy in the air.

Honoria noticed the child had dropped the comb and picked it up. "This belongs to your mother, Aideen?"

Before the child could answer, Miss Lynch snatched it out of Honoria's hand to examine it. "Oh. I seem to have made a mistake." She glared at Aideen and dropped it on the floor.

Major retrieved it and handed it to Aideen. "Here you go, sweetheart."

Aideen took it and proceeded to comb the puppy with it. She looked at Major and smiled. "This is Madigan. He's a good dog. Aren't you a good dog, Madigan?"

"Major, a gentleman does *not* sit in the middle of a hotel lobby and play with toys," Miss Lynch griped.

"If you think that, Miss Lynch, you don't know much about gentlemen." He picked up the doll and made its little arm wave at Aideen. The child burst into giggles.

"How undignified," Miss Lynch muttered. She quickly glanced around. "Where is my father?"

Honoria swallowed hard. It was now or never—she had to know. And maybe it would get rid of the horrid woman. "He went to talk to Preacher Jo."

"You mean the Reverend King?" Miss Lynch huffed.

"Yes. To set a wedding date, he said." *Well*, Honoria thought, *I always have been a glutton for punishment*.

Miss Lynch's eyes lit up. "Oh yes, of course! How silly of me!" She hiked up her skirts and headed for the door.

"Wedding?" Major asked in alarm. "What wedding?"

Miss Lynch turned as she reached the threshold. "Why ours, of course. Silly man." And she was gone.

Major scrambled to his feet, stumbled twice before he got there and ran after her.

"My doll!" Aideen cried.

Honoria sat, not knowing whether to laugh or cry. She still wasn't sure what was going on, but she had a few hints. He was attracted to her, she was certain of it. He didn't seem to think much of Miss Lynch. And if he *was* courting Miss Lynch, he didn't look like he was in as much of a hurry to marry her as she was. But that still left a lot up in the air—including the most important thing: would he ever just come out and say what his intentions were?!

"Honoria?" Aideen sobbed. "That man took Mrs. Quirk."

"Oh—yes, he did." She glanced at the doors. "Don't worry, I'm sure he'll bring her back."

"Will you get her for me?"

"He'll bring her back."

"You don't know that and I'm not allowed to leave the hotel without Mama. Mama will be mad I lost Mrs. Quirk. Please?"

Honoria got up, brushed off her skirts and nodded. "All right. I'll be back as soon as I can."

Aideen clapped. "Thank you!"

Honoria smiled. She wished she felt as enthusiastic about retrieving the blasted doll as Aideen did. But it meant following Major and Miss Lynch to the church, possibly listening to them set a date, solidifying their nuptials—or, more optimistically, a barn-burner of a screaming match if he refused to. Either way, she could think of a million other things she'd rather be doing—like chasing rattlesnakes, or being gored by a bull, or demanding Major Quincy Comfort declare his intention before she *slapped his face clean off his fool head...*

Honoria squinted her eyes shut to dispel the violent thought. Then she sighed, smiled at Aideen, and trudged out of the hotel to get Mrs. Quirk back.

Chapter Fifteen

Honoria left the boardwalk for the street, her heart thundering in her chest. This had the potential to be devastating.

Okay, so perhaps "devastating" was too strong. *So what would be a better word?* she thought as she headed toward the church. Uncomfortable? Disagreeable? Would she lose her breakfast? Not likely, but the sight of Miss Lynch nose to nose with Major in the distance did turn her stomach to a certain degree. Maybe she'd best not interrupt. Then again, if she did, she might find out more information.

"See something interesting?" She jumped as Mr. Berg stepped out of the livery stable and strolled to where she stood. He followed her gaze and folded his arms across his massive chest. "Oh, I see."

She looked up at him. "See what?"

He gave her a sideways glance. "Come now, Honoria. It's quite obvious, is it not?"

She returned her gaze to the couple arguing in front of the church. "Looks like they're having some sort of disagreement. I wonder where Preacher Jo is."

Mr. Berg shrugged. "I'm sure he's around somewhere." He pressed his lips together as his eyes flicked to the livery stable and back. "However, he is a very busy man. He could be anywhere."

"Except at the church, apparently."

He chuckled. "Maybe you should see what's the matter?"

"What? I can't interrupt. Whatever Major…er, Mr. Comfort and Miss Lynch are discussing is their private business."

He eyed her a moment. "Perhaps."

Then they both returned their attention to the two in front of the church. Miss Lynch was waving her arms around as Major stood, one hand on his hip, Aideen's doll dangling from his other. She still needed to get it, but she was still nervous about interposing herself.

Mr. Berg sighed. "I am reminded of a time when Maddie had a rival."

Honoria's head snapped around. "What?"

"Hmmm," he said with a nod. "We weren't married yet. Come to think of it, we were barely courting. A woman and her family came to town. Maddie knew them from a wagon train she and her mother had traveled with."

"Yes," she said, returning her attention to Major. "Mama told me the story."

"Everything?"

She glanced at him. "I believe so."

"Hmmm," he mused but said nothing more.

Honoria wished he'd move on. It was becoming harder and harder to watch the couple in the distance as the arm-waving (at least on Miss Lynch's part) had stopped and she had drawn closer to Major. *Much* closer. She swallowed hard. Good grief, they weren't going to kiss, were they? She didn't think she could stomach it if they… "Oh no!" Yes, they did.

"Hmmm," Mr. Berg said once more before he turned on his heel and headed for the saloon.

Tears stung the back of Honoria's eyes as she witnessed her dreams being crushed. They'd made up. It was only a matter of time before their wedding would take place. With a heavy heart she turned and walked toward the Triple-C's wagon, not looking back. She wanted nothing more to do with Major and everything to do with planning her trip abroad. The sooner she got started, the better.

"Uncle Colin?" Honoria said on the way home.

"Yes, poppet?"

"I want to visit Uncle Duncan. Will you help me convince Papa I can go?"

"I don't see a problem with that. Just the other day your mother mentioned you visiting them to your aunt."

"She did?" Honoria was surprised—she'd brought it up to her mother just the one time. She had no idea the conversation had already set things in motion. Maybe this wouldn't be as hard as she first thought. She clutched her hands and rested them in her lap. "I could travel with the Bergs."

"Yes, I suppose," he said, his eyes fixed on the road ahead. "But tell me, why this sudden interest to see your aunt and uncle?"

Her mouth went dry as a chill raced up her spine. "Well… I've been thinking about England. I've not been since I was a child."

"A baby," he corrected.

"And people keep telling me that I need to grow up, that I should act more like a lady. But here I am out on the edge of nowhere, and I know Mama and Auntie Belle try their best, but…it's not easy to learn proper etiquette out here. I love Clear Creek, really I do, but if I'm going to learn how to truly be a lady, wouldn't Stantham or London be a better place for me?"

"Yes, of course" Uncle Colin smiled at her. "You've really been giving this some thought."

She licked her lips and nodded. The image of Major kissing Miss Lynch had lodged itself in her brain, and it was all she could do to keep the picture at bay. "When are the Bergs leaving?"

He glanced at her with a smile. "You sound as if you're in a hurry."

Honoria looked away, her eyes awash with unshed tears. "No time like the present, I suppose." She swallowed hard, lest she start to sob. She'd let Major and Miss Lynch's kiss get to her. But there was nothing she could do about it. Things were what they were. Miss Lynch came to Clear Creek to get married to him, so why shouldn't she?

Besides, Honoria had no claim on the man. All she'd done was flirt with him and share a few horse rides. She wasn't a refined Southern lady like Miss Lynch; she just knew how to hold her temper better, as was obvious from the comb incident. Speaking of which, she hoped Major had returned Aideen her doll. She felt guilty about not getting it back for the child, but she just couldn't stomach watching Major and Miss Lynch anymore. For all she knew, the next time she went to town they'd be married.

But that's not how things normally went around Clear Creek. The ladies' sewing circle would want to help the woman sew a wedding dress. A huge wedding supper would be planned and the entire town would want to attend the ceremony.

Normally. She had a feeling Miss Lynch wanted to get married yesterday and would see it done as soon as possible.

"Poppet?"

Honoria wiped her eyes and faced forward. "What?"

"Why do you really want to visit Duncan and Cozette?"

"Because I want..." She stopped. What could she tell him?

"Yes?"

Her heart felt like it was breaking, but that was ridiculous. Why should it? She wiped at her eyes again. "Because I want Uncle Duncan to find me a husband!" she blurted with more force than intended.

"Oh! Well, that sheds some extra light on the matter."

Honoria unconsciously smoothed her skirt. "Does it?"

"I'll have to speak with your father. I can tell you right now, he's not going to like it."

"How do you know? Wouldn't he rather see me married to an English gentleman?"

"I have nothing against it, and I'm sure neither will Harrison. But it means you'll be gone from Clear Creek."

She drew in a deep breath. "Yes. I know."

"England?" Harrison exclaimed at the supper table. "Marriage?"

Honoria watched her father with bated breath. The man looked ready to explode.

And did. He stood so fast he knocked his chair over. "You can't get married!"

Sadie shook her head. "For Heaven's sake, Harrison, sit down!" she scolded.

"After you pick up your chair, of course," Colin added.

Honoria sat quietly. She'd let her parents battle it out first, then put in her own reasoning.

Her father picked up his chair, righted it, but didn't sit. "What's all this talk of marriage?"

"She's eighteen, Harrison," Sadie scolded. "She's of age."

"What's the rush?" He held out both hands. "I don't see why she would want to hurry into such a…a…"

"A what?" Sadie also stood. "And don't you dare say 'travesty'."

"I-I-I had no such word in mind."

"Then what?" she demanded.

Harrison's eyes darted around the table. They were in the formal dining room with Aunt Belle and Uncle Colin, Logan and Susara, while Edith and Jefferson managed the children in the kitchen. After a moment, he finally settled on Honoria. "Why on earth do you want to marry?"

She shrugged. "It seems like the prudent thing to do."

"Prudent?!" His face turned an interesting shade of red. "Prudent, she says! Well I never!"

"Harrison…" Sadie warned, sounding like she'd had about enough of this.

"Don't you 'Harrison' me, wife! I'm tired of everyone's nonsense!"

Honoria lost it. "And I'm tired of yours!"

Harrison's face froze. "What did you say?"

"You heard me, Papa! You keep telling me I need to grow up, but you never let me! Now I want to go to England to learn to be a proper lady and find a proper husband, and you…you…" She stood, fighting to keep the tears at bay. "If I'm not old enough now, when will I be? Do you really want me to grow up, or do you want me to stay a child here forever?"

Harrison stared at her in stunned silence. She'd never talked back to him like this before, not with such intensity—or such logic.

"Honoria, sit down," her mother said, her voice calm now.

"Uncle Colin," said Honoria. "Tell him."

"Tell me what?" Harrison asked as his eyes met those of her uncle's.

"She wants to go, brother. And I think you'll agree, her reasons are sound. You remember what it was like for us at that age."

"We were tending pigs, working so we wouldn't starve," Harrison stated.

"Exactly!" Colin replied. "We did our best to be gentlemen, but you and I both know we could have used help."

"Still do," Belle quipped.

"I wish you were wrong, dear. And by the grace of God, we ended up with wonderful wives. But who does Honoria have to marry around Clear Creek—farmboys and laborers? The Comforts are the most cultured among them, and they're all poor as church mice—they can't take care of her. And as the eldest has shown, they can't restrain her… well, less ladylike impulses. No offense, poppet."

"None taken," Honoria sighed. The last thing she'd wanted from this was another reminder of Major.

Now Sadie jumped in. "And what is she learning about being a proper lady around here? I do my best, husband, but I'm just a hard-working west Texas cattleman's daughter. And all she gets to do is help me around the house, do a few outside chores, run some errands. Maxwell and Clinton are old enough to handle those."

"Speaking for myself, I don't think I want to try any of my nephew's cooking," Colin said.

"I'll second that," Logan tossed in.

"You're getting us off track, boys," Sadie grumbled, then turned back to Harrison. "Is this really all you want for our daughter? She wants the chance to be what you've always said you want her to be. Surely you can see that."

Honoria sat and waited.

Harrison looked at the ceiling and mumbled something—

a prayer, perhaps?—then rubbed his chin a few times as he so often did when flustered. "I'll write to your uncle in England. But! You'll agree to whatever travel arrangements your mother and I make."

Honoria's eyes shifted between her parents. "That's agreeable."

"It had better be," her father said sternly. "Sadie?"

Honoria's mother nodded. "All right. We'll discuss the particulars later."

Honoria swallowed hard. "And marriage?"

"Egads, girl!" her father cried. "One thing at a time."

Honoria sat. She'd won the first round. Now all she had to do was convince them to let her leave with the Bergs. If they were planning on leaving just after Christmas… good heavens! She'd forgotten all about Christmas, and it was only about two weeks away! No wonder she'd hadn't seen Preacher Jo around town—he was probably immersed in the annual Christmas play. For all she knew, he'd been at the hotel talking with Mr. Van Cleet about it while she and Major were…

"Major…"

"What was that?" Aunt Belle asked.

"Nothing," Honoria said. "I…just remembered Christmas is coming."

"Yes, and we have to start getting busy," Sadie said. "Annie and Preacher Jo will be here tomorrow to discuss our participation."

"Participation?" Harrison squeaked. "It's that time of year already?"

"Preacher Jo seems to be getting a late start on things this year," Colin said.

"We're doing things a little different this time around," Susara offered. "A Christmas concert. Since most everyone in town knows the music, we don't have to have as many rehearsals and more people can get involved."

"You mean there's not going to be a play?!" Harrison asked.

"Oh bother," Colin said. "And I was so looking forward to seeing Andel in his tree costume again."

Belle snorted. "Oh my goodness, no!"

Logan and Susara laughed. "What a sight that was back in the day!" Logan said.

Honoria had heard that story. Poor Mr. Berg got to be a tree in almost every scene of Clear Creek's first Christmas play—and managed to clobber a couple of outlaws while in costume!

"Enough about the play, concert, whatever you're doing," Harrison said. "I want no more discussion of anything! I'd like to finish my meal!"

"You already did," Sadie pointed out.

Harrison studied his empty plate. "Oh. So I did."

"Dessert?" Belle stood. Sadie and Susara did as well and headed for the kitchen.

Honoria did the same. She'd had enough conversation with her father for one night. Besides, with Christmas close at hand, she wanted to enjoy what time she had left. Who knew—if she left for England with the Bergs, she could be married by this time next year. If so, this could very well be her last Christmas at the Triple-C for a very long time.

"Daddy, the man was horrible, just horrible!"

"What do you mean?" Archibald asked as he gave his daughter a good once-over. He'd never seen her so angry.

"He outright *spurned* me!" she screeched, stomping her foot.

"Oh dear, dear, dear. That does muddle things, doesn't it?"

Tears streamed down Lucretia's face. "Why can't that

man see *reason*? What's wrong with being married to li'l ol' me? He's been leading me *on*!"

Archibald sighed heavily. "My, my, we can't have that now, can we?"

"*Do something!*" Lucretia demanded with another stomp. "I won't be so humiliated!"

Things were not going as he planned. "You'll get over it, my dear. What troubles me is, you still need to get married."

"And how am I supposed to do that when *he* doesn't want to?"

"What exactly did you do?"

"I didn't do anything! I had Major right there at the church, but that silly reverend wasn't anywhere in sight! How could I plead my case with an absent clergyman?"

"That's strange. I saw him not moments before you and your Mr. Comfort came along." Archibald began to pace. "Most strange."

"I saw the church doors were open and thought someone was just inside. That's when I kissed Major. A lot of good it did!"

Archibald stopped pacing and smiled. "I like how you think on your feet, my dear. Too bad no one witnessed it."

"If anyone did, they paid it no mind." She flounced into a nearby chair. "That Cooke girl, for one—she saw me do it and didn't do a thing."

"Good. Let her think you're getting married. Maybe she'll stay out of our hair from now on."

"That barbaric-looking stranger in town also saw us."

"Mr. Berg?" Archibald said with delight. "How wonderful!"

"How is that wonderful?"

"From what I've observed, the people in this town respect him. That being said, what if *he* thought you'd been compromised?"

"You mean, more so than the Rev. King?"

"Precisely, my dear. There are folks here who'd demand you and Mr. Comfort marry. Then all our problems would be solved."

"I don't know, Daddy. I still think it would've been better if the reverend witnessed it."

"Did Mr. Comfort, er…enjoy it? If so, maybe a marriage proposal is still at hand."

Lucretia crossed her arms in front of her and pouted. "No! I tried to hang onto him for as long as I could, but he shoved me away! I've never been so embarrassed in my life! The nerve of him!"

"Now, now, my dear," her father cooed. "You'll get your man. You just leave it to Daddy. That and good timing."

"Timing?"

"Why, yes. It's all a matter of being in the right place at the right time with the right people around to witness your…" He smiled. "…plunge into debauchery."

"Debauchery!"

"Fallen state," he corrected. "At the hands of none other than Major Comfort, of course."

She relaxed and smiled. "That sounds better."

"I knew it would. Now you get a good night's sleep, my dear. In the morning I'll work on a plan. In the meantime, why don't you get out more, meet some of the other women in town? Make it appear as if you're settling in. People would be more apt to be on your side when the time comes."

Lucretia bit her bottom lip as she thought. "Yes, I suppose I could suffer through one of those sewing circle things. I think there's one tomorrow."

"You do that." He scratched his head. "Come to think

of it, why don't you take a look around that mercantile and see if there's something you fancy for Christmas? It'll be here before we know it."

"There's only one thing I want for Christmas, Daddy—and that's Major Comfort."

Her father grinned like the Devil. "Consider it done."

Chapter Sixteen

Over the next several days, Honoria kept to herself and tried to stay out of her father's way. But he was also staying out of hers—whether on purpose or simply because he was busy, she had no idea. He always seemed to be discussing the ranch with her uncle, with Logan, even with Grandpa Jefferson. She was just happy she didn't have to converse with him much, even at mealtimes.

To further the gap between them, she agreed to help Susara with the Christmas concert. It was an easy enough task—she already knew who in Clear Creek could carry a tune and who sounded like a dying goose. Still, Preacher Jo and Annie wanted to hold auditions tomorrow, and start rehearsals a few days after that. This would give those participating a mere ten days to prepare.

But as Susara reminded her the other night at supper, everyone already knew the music. The townsfolk had sung the hymns every Christmas for years—they'd just make a bigger show of it this year. Why Preacher Jo didn't want to put on a play she couldn't guess. Maybe he just wanted to change things up.

"Did your mother tell you that Miss Lynch came to the

sewing circle?" Aunt Belle asked as she took some biscuits out of the oven.

Honoria stared at her a moment, then remembered to breathe. "She did?"

Aunt Belle put the biscuits on the worktable and wiped her brow with the back of her hand. "Yes. She was quite cordial, actually. Looks like she'll be joining us from now on."

Honoria shivered. "How nice," she said, hoping it didn't sound forced. Thank heavens she'd be leaving soon. Speaking of which… "Auntie Belle?"

"Yes?" She put another batch of biscuits in the oven and closed the door.

"You wouldn't happen to know if Mama spoke with Uncle Colin and Papa about England, would you?"

"As in you going?" her aunt teased. "No, I'm sorry—I haven't heard a word. Why don't you ask them?"

"I will. I just thought that maybe if you'd heard something…"

"You'd have a better idea of what their plans were?" she finished. "Or you wouldn't have to face your father about it."

Honoria shrugged. "Both."

Her aunt went to a nearby hutch, took out two cups and saucers, put them on the worktable and reached for the coffee pot on the stove. "Honoria, do you really want to go to England that badly?"

Honoria waited for her aunt to pour, then took a cup and saucer and headed for the kitchen table. "Of course I do. With the Bergs here, I think it's the perfect time. Don't they have to go through England to get to their country? Papa can't argue about having them as an escort." She sat.

"No, it would work well. There's no safer people to be with than the Bergs and their guard, and Maddie would be good company. But I thought...perhaps you might have a reason to stay," her aunt added hesitantly.

Honoria began to fidget in her chair. "What reason would that be?"

"A certain Southern gentleman?"

Honoria's stomach fluttered. Oh good grief, Aunt Belle hadn't even said his name! "That's not really a reason to *stay*," she snapped. "Seeing as that certain Southern gentleman is marrying Miss Lynch."

"Yes, I gathered as much from her conversation at the sewing circle."

"Then why would I stay here for him?" Honoria had to bite her lower lip to keep it from trembling. "Have they set a date?"

"We were so busy discussing her dress, no one thought to ask. But as I recall, there was no rush."

Honoria took a quick sip of her coffee.

"You liked him, didn't you?" Aunt Belle asked matter-of-factly.

Honoria almost choked. "Perhaps a little. But I'm not stupid, Auntie—"

"I didn't say you were."

"—I mean, Miss Lynch came here as a mail-order bride to marry Mr. Comfort. Naturally they'd do so." She took another sip. "Who am I to interfere?"

"That's wise," her aunt said. "Perhaps I've misjudged Mr. Comfort."

"What do you mean?"

"When he came to supper with the Bergs, we all thought...oh, never mind."

"No, what did you think?"

Her aunt took a drink of her own coffee, then shrugged. "From the looks of it, he gave every indication he wanted to court *you*. Even Maddie and Andel thought so. I must say, I'm rather disappointed in the man. It wasn't right for him to give you false hope."

"Auntie Belle, I'm not *desperate*."

Her aunt smiled and nodded. "I know. But I wouldn't blame you for being disappointed."

Touché. Apparently she wasn't as good as she thought when it came to hiding her emotions from family. Honoria blew a loose wisp of hair off her face. "I am, a little," she lied. "But he's not for me. He still lives at the men's camp, for one—do you really think Papa would let him court me knowing that?"

Belle studied her a moment. "If your father knew he really loved you, then yes, I believe he would."

Honoria gaped. "Do you really think so?"

Aunt Belle smiled. "I believe I know so. But only if you felt the same about him."

She closed her eyes, not caring if her expression gave her emotions away. "Well, it doesn't matter now, does it? He's marrying Miss Lynch, and I'm going to England. Who knows when I'll be back anyway?"

Aunt Belle nodded. "Yes. Who knows?"

The next day Honoria, accompanied Logan and Susara into town to help with the auditions. Everyone who'd played a part in previous Christmas plays showed up, plus a few families who were normally in the audience. Some women were quick to volunteer their husbands (who were out working) to take part as well. Honoria wondered how many of the men knew what their wives were up to. They'd find out soon enough.

Right now, she had to find someone to take charge of organizing the refreshments. Mrs. Dunnigan and Mrs. Upton still baked for such occasions, but preferred to leave the managing of the tables to the younger women. Honoria herself oversaw the cookie table last year. Maybe she'd do it again this year—if she was stuck behind a refreshment table, she'd reduce the risk of bumping into Major or his betrothed.

Hmmm, she mused. *I wonder what kind of cookies Major likes...no! Stop thinking about him!* Maybe she ought to make sure they had all the cookies he *didn't* like, so he'd stay away.

"Honoria?" Susara called as she approached. "Do you think you can manage the children?"

"Children?" Thank Heaven, something else to think about!

"Yes, they're going to be singing a few hymns by themselves. Most of them already know them—it's more a matter of helping them to stay in tune."

"Are you saying you want me to conduct?"

"Yes. Can you?"

Honoria's chest warmed at the thought. It was the first time something had made her feel good since she saw Major and Miss Lynch—*shudder*—kiss. "Yes, I'd love to."

"Wonderful!" Susara was off again.

"Congratulations."

Honoria went cold, enough to have to wrap her arms around herself. *Oh no, not now*, she thought. She was standing in the center aisle near the back of the church, facing the front, and hadn't even heard the doors open behind her.

"You must be an accomplished singer to be put in charge of such a task," Major said as he came around to stand in front of her.

"I can carry a tune," she said stiffly. He gazed at her but kept silent. Infuriating—why did he have to torture her like this? "Did you need something, Mr. Comfort?" she finally asked, just wanting him to go away.

"No, Miss Cooke," he said with a weary sigh, twisting his hat in his hands. "I suppose not."

His brothers entered the church behind him. "There you are, Quince!" exclaimed one of them—Michael, was it? He approached and slapped Major on the back. "This should be fun." He glanced at Honoria. "Miss Cooke, how nice to see you."

The rest of the Comfort men seated themselves in the nearby pews and took off their hats. "Mrs. Kincaid will be with you in a moment," Honoria informed them. "She's the one assigning parts."

"Major here has a lovely baritone voice," Michael volunteered. "I'm sure you'll love it once you hear it." Major sent him an icy glare, but Michael ignored it. "Do you sing, Miss Cooke?"

She noticed the rest of Major's brothers were staring at her. "I'll be conducting the children," she said neutrally.

"I can't tell you how much we've been looking forward to this," another—Darcy?—said. "Mr. Mulligan and Sheriff Turner have been talking about it for days."

"They do that every year," she told him. "You should've seen it when Sheriff Hughes was here."

"I understand this is the first year he's not," Major said, breaking his silence. He was staring at her with an intensity she hadn't seen before.

Against her will, something warmed deep within her, and she didn't know whether to turn and run or throw herself into his arms. The latter made no sense—he was getting married soon and that was that. The sooner she got away from him, the better off she'd be.

Just then, the church doors opened. Thank heaven the Bergs had arrived, giving her an excuse to part company with Major and his brothers. "If you'll excuse me, I need to speak with Maddie Berg."

"It was a pleasure speaking with you," Major said in his deep Southern drawl.

Honoria thought her insides were going to pool on the floor. Why, why, *why* did he have such an effect on her? More importantly, why didn't he go pester somebody else? "I have to go," she squeaked. She turned, locked eyes with Maddie and made for her. Was it just her imagination or could she actually *feel* Major's eyes follow her retreat?

The look in Maddie's eyes said her instincts were true. So did the woman's first words, even before "hello."

"Why does Mr. Comfort have such a funny look on his face?"

Honoria knew she shouldn't, but turned and looked anyway. He stood, unmoving, gawking at her. "I have no idea." She spun to Maddie. "Susara put me in charge of the children. Would you like to help?"

"Certainly! Anything we can do."

Mr. Berg glanced warily between Honoria and Major as he tapped his fingers against his hip. "Hmmm..."

Other than Major's voice, the last thing Honoria wanted to hear right now was Mr. Berg humming. She grabbed Maddie by the hand and pulled her up the side aisle of the church to avoid walking past Major and his brothers. Near the front Susara and Mrs. Mulligan were herding the children into a corner. Susara told them which hymns the children would sing, then went to assign parts to the Comfort brothers.

"Well, look what the cat dragged in," Mrs. Mulligan remarked. "I must say, they're a handsome lot."

Honoria was confused, then realized the woman wasn't talking about the youngsters—she was talking about the Comforts. She rolled her eyes.

"I wonder if they can sing?"

"I'm sure they can, or they wouldn't be here," Maddie

remarked. "I can't tell you how excited I am to do this. Things are so different in Dalrovia—the country is very set in its ways, including its music. This will be a nice change."

Honoria smiled, nodded, did her best not to look at Major…and failed. He stood listening to Susara, but his eyes were still fixed on Honoria. A thrill ran up her spine, whispering that he was unable to take his eyes off her. But in her mind, she wished he would—hadn't he strung her along enough?

"Aye," Mrs. Mulligan agreed. "Well, shall we get to work, kiddies?" she told the children assembled around them.

Honoria saw Major's eyes soften, as if inviting her to join him where he stood. She took a step in his direction before she caught herself, swallowed hard and faced Maddie and Mrs. Mulligan. "Yes, children, let's get started." Just as well—Miss Lynch had entered and was making a beeline for Major. "Let's go into the church office where we won't be disturbed by everyone else," she added.

"Won't it be too cramped in there?" Mrs. Mulligan asked.

"We'll make it work. Let's go." Honoria headed for the office, the kids trailing behind. How was she going to get through this? It seemed every time she laid eyes on the man, her heart sunk a little deeper in love with him. And that way lay only more pain, more aggravation. *God in heaven, just get me through this and far, far away from here,* she prayed silently as she walked.

"What do you think, Major?" Miss Lynch asked. "Are you willing to bury the hatchet, as they say?" He looked at her over the back of the pew as she fanned herself, looking quite demure. He knew better—the woman was a harpy, manipulative, self-centered, annoying, a walking reminder of every grasping society belle he'd gladly left behind in Savannah. Women like that were a major reason he was still unwed at nearly thirty years of age.

It'd been almost a week since his brief conversation with Honoria at the auditions, and he hadn't been able to get her out of his mind since. Making peace with Lucretia Lynch would only make it harder—mainly because he wouldn't have the bothersome woman to distract him from Honoria. His whole body tightened at the mere thought.

"Major, are you listening to me?"

He slowly turned back to her, realizing he'd twisted away to scan the church for a sign of the one person he wanted to talk to but couldn't find. "Not really. I'm sorry, Miss Lynch."

"Oh fiddle-dee-dee. After all we've been through together, surely you can call me Lucretia. After all, I've been calling you Major for weeks."

He smiled coldly. "So you have, Miss Lynch, so you have."

That had the expected reaction. "Oh! You are so frustrating! Can I help it if…well, call it whatever you want! But I certainly do hope your daddy is ashamed of what he's done! Have you heard back from him *yet*?"

"Oddly, no. I haven't."

"You don't think that…" She put a hand over her mouth. "Lord forbid, but you don't think that he's passed on, do you?"

His eyes widened. "Miss Lynch, I'll ask you not to even suggest such a thing, especially in the presence of my brothers," he told her sharply.

She batted her eyelashes at him. "Well, I do apologize, but one has to think of these things. Why else would he not write?"

"A good question. But if he'd fallen into ill health, my aunt would've let us know."

"I see." Suddenly she looked past him.

He turned to see what had gotten her attention—Honoria! She emerged from the church office with several children in tow, went to Annie King the preacher's wife and started speaking with her. His heart skipped at the sight of her. He wanted—no, *needed* to speak with her!

"I envy that woman," Lucretia said.

Involuntarily, he turned. "Miss Cooke?"

She gave him a calculating look. "Now how would you know if I was talking about her?"

He shrugged. "Lucky guess," he answered dryly.

She rolled her eyes. "Why, Major, here I traveled all this way to marry you, only to find that some local farm girl caught your eye."

"Miss Lynch, I warn you to speak more kindly of the people here. Some of them are friends."

She smiled again, with a flutter of lashes. "Well, that *friend* of yours is headed to England, so I hear."

"England?!" Major felt his heart sink into his shoes. Honoria was leaving? He pressed his lips together and put his hands in his pockets, lest Lucretia see his clenched fists. "I...hadn't heard that."

"It's all the talk of the sewing circle. The Bergs are escorting her there shortly after Christmas."

Major's gut twisted into knots. Honoria was leaving Clear Creek, leaving him. He'd spent the last week agonizing over how to approach her and her family. He wanted to court her eventually, but knew that after all that had happened he'd have to prove himself first. Not to mention show her father he could work hard, save his money and have enough to take care of his daughter one day. Now it looked as if he might not get the chance.

"Major, are you all right? You've gone pale."

Did Lucretia actually look concerned about someone besides herself? He must look horrid indeed. "I'm fine. A bit tired, perhaps."

"What's goin' on with ya two?" Jasper Kiggins asked as he joined them. "Ya as excited about the performance as I am?"

"Hello, Jasper," Major said as his eyes drifted back to Honoria and Mrs. King. He wanted to go to her, take her in his arms and tell her all the reasons why she couldn't go to England. How he'd thought of nothing but her, how he couldn't fight what was in his heart any longer. He wanted her more than he'd wanted anything since he'd survived the war. But what did it matter? He had nothing to offer, not a penny to his name. She was better off going abroad. A blessing, really.

Maybe by the time she got back he'd have enough money saved…if she came back. And if she didn't find a man in England who could give her the life she deserved. Her uncle was an honest-to-goodness duke, after all—there were probably plenty of suitable gentlemen in his circle.

He caught Lucretia studying him out the corner of one eye. "Is there something else you wanted?"

"Not that I'm ever likely to get. You go about your business and I'll go about mine." She smiled oddly, making him flinch, then stood and sashayed down the aisle to speak with Ada Brody. He hoped that meant she was prepared to drop once and for all this business of marrying him.

"She sure is purty," Jasper whispered beside him.

"Yes, she is. But…"

"But what? She ain't ornery, is she? Cain't stand ornery women."

"She's…well…" Major turned to look at Honoria, but

she was gone. She must've retreated back to the church office to work with the children. "Blast," he sighed.

"What's the matter?" Jasper asked.

"Nothing. I'll see you back at the men's camp." Major left, not caring if he was missed.

Chapter Seventeen

"Are you packed?" Honoria's mother asked as she came into her room.

"Not yet."

Sadie sat on the bed next to her. "Why not? You leave shortly after Christmas."

Honoria took a deep breath. Christmas was only two days away, and she'd immersed herself so deeply into the town's Christmas concert, she'd hardly had time to think. Intentionally—it kept thoughts of Major at bay. She hadn't caught more than a glimpse of him lately, and hadn't seen Miss Lynch (who wasn't involved in the singing) at all.

"Honoria, are you all right?"

She dared not look at her mother, knowing what it would do to her.

"Honoria?"

Her lower lip began to tremble and before she knew it, she was lost.

"Honoria!"

"Oh Mama…"

Sadie wrapped her arms around her. "Sweetling, what's wrong?"

"Nothing. Everything."

"You're not making sense," Sadie gently pushed them apart. "What is it? Have you changed your mind about England?"

Honoria shook her head. "No, I *have* to go."

"What do you mean, *have* to go?"

She straightened, wiped her eyes and swallowed hard. "I'm fine."

Sadie sighed. "No, you're not. But when you're ready to tell me, I'm here."

Honoria sniffed, nodded and stood. Her mother knew her all too well. Best retreat while she could. "I have to go to Dunnigan's Mercantile. I've hardly made any gifts."

"Do you need money?"

"I have some, thank you."

Sadie eyed her. "Fine. I'll see if anyone's around to drive you."

"I'd rather ride. It'd be quicker."

Sadie gave her a stern look.

"I won't race anyone, if that's what you're thinking."

"All right. Can you get me some cinnamon while you're there? I'm almost out."

"Yes, I can."

Sadie stood. "I wish you'd tell me what's wrong."

Honoria's eyes filled with tears again. Curse that Major Comfort—for her, he was anything but! He was making her life miserable without even being around. To make matters worse, Miss Lynch was quickly gaining friends in town. She'd been spending a lot of time helping Lucy White out with the Christmas food preparations, and Preacher Jo mentioned she wanted to volunteer at the church after the holiday. The thought turned Honoria's stomach. Well, at least by then she'd have left for England.

"If you're going to go, you'd better hurry," Sadie suggested.

"Yes, Mama, I know," she said with all the enthusiasm of someone going to the gallows.

Sadie took one last look at her, shook her head in dismay and left the bedroom.

As soon as she was gone, Honoria sighed in resignation, gathered what she needed and headed off to saddle Rowley. The ride to town was quiet and cold—it had snowed a little every day for the last two weeks, and the landscape was muffled in white drifts. No one was out on the road—or in the mercantile except Mrs. Dunnigan. She didn't feel like talking to anyone, so this suited her fine.

"Good morning," Mrs. Dunnigan huffed. "What do you need?"

"Mama needs some cinnamon, and I need to get some Christmas gifts."

"You sure waited 'til the last minute."

Honoria smiled. She liked how Irene Dunnigan spoke her mind and got away with it. "I know. I also know you have things my brothers and sister would want."

"Better get to it, then. There's some new hair ribbons in Savannah would like."

"Good—I'll take a look." She knew where the ribbons were displayed and went straight to them. She picked out two green, a blue and a red, and set them on the counter.

"That Major Comfort was just in here," Mrs. Dunnigan remarked.

Honoria paled.

Mrs. Dunnigan scrunched up her face, narrowed her eyes and looked Honoria over top to bottom. "Uh-huh. Thought so."

"Thought...what?"

"Younguns," she remarked in disgust.

"You thought what?! Consarnit, just say it!" Honoria

could speak her mind too; she just suffered for it more than Mrs. Dunnigan seemed to.

The matron leaned across the counter, her eyes intense. "You're in love."

Honoria reeled back. "I am not!"

Mrs. Dunnigan smirked and nodded. "Uh-*huh.* I'll get your cinnamon."

Tears stung the back of Honoria's eyes as Irene turned away. She put a hand to her mouth to stifle a sob. *Yes!* she screamed in her head. *Yes, I AM in love, so much I want to die!* The thought of Major and Miss Lynch marrying soon made her feel like she was walking to her own demise. Each day brought her closer, closer, until finally she'd be no more.

"Need anything else?" Mrs. Dunnigan asked as she straightened and turned around, a tiny bag in her hand. She twisted it, tied it closed with string and set it on the counter. "You know, he talked about you while he was here—said he'll be sorry to see you go. England's a long ways off."

Honoria opened her mouth but couldn't find her voice, and was afraid to say anything regardless lest she start sobbing. Her emotions were out of control at this point. She needed to take care of business and leave as soon as she could. She turned and headed for the other side of the mercantile to find gifts for her brothers.

"I ain't much of a romantic—that's Wilfred's department. But he sure looked like a man in love."

Honoria grabbed a display table for support. Was the woman *trying* to hurt her?

"You know, I don't like that Lynch woman. Reminds me too much of those plantation women back in Alabama, always looking down their noses at us normal folks. But I suppose she has her reasons…"

"Stop!" Honoria yelled from across the store. "Enough! I don't want to hear any more."

Mrs. Dunnigan came out from behind the counter. "Then what are you going to do about it?" she barked back.

Honoria stood, stunned. What was she talking about? She turned, grabbed a small hunting knife and scabbard and two books, marched to the counter and slammed them down. "I'll take these."

Mrs. Dunnigan picked up one of the books. "*Alice's Adventures in Wonderland*," she read. "You sure Clinton's gonna like this? I know he's a big reader and all, but…"

"It'll be fine! How much?"

Mrs. Dunnigan stared at her. "Honoria Cooke, you are a stubborn, spoilt girl."

Honoria gasped. "What?!"

"You heard me. You've wanted for nothing all your life, and now when it comes time to give something to someone, you get stingy."

Honoria backed up a step and shook her head, her mind reeling. What was she talking about? Had Mrs. Dunnigan finally gone around the bend? Or maybe *she* had…

"Don't look at me like that—you know it's true. Forgive them and move on!"

"Forgive? Forgive who?"

"Mr. Comfort and that Lynch woman."

Honoria's lower lip started in again. *Oh no...*

"And another thing—"

"Stop, please…"

"—spoiled and stubborn you may be, but this is the only time I've ever thought you cowardly!"

That got her attention. Honoria opened her tear-filled eyes, only just realizing she'd closed them. "What do you mean?" came out barely a whisper.

"Honey, you want something, you go after it. For the life

of me I can't figure out why you haven't—unless it's because you haven't forgiven that man for being such a fool."

"What?" Honoria was completely lost at this point and just wanted to leave.

"You heard me. Consorting with the likes of that Lynch woman—What. An. Idiot. And now you're going to England and he's going to Denver!"

Honoria's eyes went wide. "Denver?"

"To check on his pa. They ain't heard from him, not even after writing twice. No one's heard from that mail-order bride establishment neither. So it ain't all Miss Lynch's fault, you see, even if I do think she's a tarted-up shrew."

Honoria swallowed hard. Oh—*now* she understood! Major wasn't making her life miserable—*she* was. Her suffering was her fault, because while she'd fallen in love with the man, she'd done nothing about it except become angry and miserable and plan to run away. In short, being cowardly. Mrs. Dunnigan was right—she did need to forgive Major and Miss Lynch, let them marry and move on, not work herself into a state because she wanted something she couldn't have.

"Oh my Lord," she whispered. Mrs. Dunnigan had backed her into a corner and let her have it. And it was just what she'd needed.

"Well?" Mrs. Dunnigan huffed.

Honoria let the tears fall as she smiled at the cantankerous old woman. "Oh, Mrs. Dunnigan, thank you."

"I'll pay you back as soon as I'm able," Major said while packing his carpetbag. He and Andel Berg were at the men's camp, from which Major would soon be leaving to catch the next stage out of town thanks to Andel's generous loan. His eventual destination was Denver, to check on his father and see what the story behind Lucretia Lynch's arrival was. Very few people knew he was going, but soon all of Clear Creek would, since he'd told Irene Dunnigan that morning. Once she told Fanny Fig, everyone would know. Including Honoria.

A tiny smirk formed on Andel's face. "That you will."

Major looked at him. "You make that sound like a threat."

"Consider it a promise."

He shoved a few more small items into the bag. "My brother Michael is the best one to speak with if you still want to investigate introducing different crops into your country. You'll find him most intelligent."

"If he's anything like you, I'm sure he is. In fact, all your brothers look to be very capable."

"Matt could use some smoothing out, but he's young," Major cautioned.

"Not for long. The prairie has a way of turning boys into men. Good men, for the most part." Andel shifted his weight as he stood, making the floor of the cabin creak.

"You'll give my regards to your wife?"

"Yes, of course." Andel rocked again.

"Is something wrong?"

"Don't you find it a little strange that not only your letters to this Mrs. Pettigrew, but Mr. Lynch's letters as well, never made it?"

"We don't know that for sure. For all we know Mrs. Pettigrew is slow to respond."

"Not to me she wasn't."

Major stopped what he was doing and looked at him. "What?"

"I sent her a letter. And got a prompt reply." Andel reached into his coat pocket and pulled out an envelope. "From the Pettigrew Bridal Agency." He handed it to Major.

Major took it, pulled out the letter and began to read.

Your esteemed Royal Highness:

Andel shrugged. "The title has its perks. I'm surprised she didn't send a telegraph, but since Clear Creek doesn't have its own office..."

Major returned to the letter.

I'm sorry for any misunderstanding on the part of Mr. Major Comfort. I am acquainted with his sister Pleasant, who used my services some months ago to procure a husband. I hear from her now and then, and am happy to know she is blissfully wed.

He looked at Andel. "She is, you know."

"So I've heard. Read on. I think you'll find the next part quite interesting."

To answer your question, I've never met or heard from a Buford Comfort, only his daughter, who was accompanied to my office by a different relative, a Miss Phidelia Hamilton.

Major looked up from the letter. "What does this mean?"

"Keep reading..."

Major's jaw muscles began to twitch as he continued.

Regarding the matter of Miss Lucretia Lynch. A woman by that name, accompanied by her father, did seek my services several months ago, but did not find the applicants I had on hand to their liking. I have not seen them since.

I hope this helps. I'm sorry if the information is sparse, but that is all I know.

Au revoir,
Mme. Adelia Pettigrew

P.S. Give my regards to Her Majesty the Queen. I hope to visit your country someday.

Major's throat tightened. He wanted to crush the paper in his hand, but it was the only proof he had that…good grief! He looked at Andel. "What are those two trying to pull?!"

"Mr. Lynch and his daughter? A very good question." Andel crossed his arms over his chest. "I like a good mystery as much as the next, but when it involves family I am no longer amused."

"Family?"

"Honoria Cooke."

Major gulped. "You're related to the Cookes?"

"Not by blood, but by vow. I swore an oath to protect my wife no matter the cost. When I did, it was simply duty, but has since become something else entirely. While living here, that vow extended to the Cooke family, and as far as I'm concerned still does. They have been like family to me, as have the Wallers, and through them the Drakes." A wry smile formed on the big man's lips.

"Lynch mailed my letters along with his own," Major thought aloud.

"Did he?"

"Or not," Major made a fist. He wanted to hit something, or someone. Any angrier and he'd risk hitting Andel, which wouldn't be the wisest thing to do. Archibald Lynch, on the other hand…

"Tell me one thing," Andel said, interrupting his thoughts.

"What?"

"If Miss Lynch hadn't claimed to be your mail-order bride, would you have pursued Honoria?"

"Pursued her? I beg your pardon, Your Highness, but I don't see where that's any of your…oh, right. Family, you said. But what makes you think I had any interest in…?"

"Oh come now, Mr. Comfort. Anyone with eyes could see."

"Truly?"

"Truly," Andel said with a grin. "May I offer some advice?"

Major could finish packing and walk away, but the brute would catch him in two strides. Besides, given how he'd clearly been bamboozled by the Lynches, he could probably use all the wisdom he could get. "Certainly."

"Don't take the stage today. It's Christmas Eve, and you should spend the holiday with your family, not in some lonely stage stop. And there's no rush to get to your father now."

Major stared at the carpet bag on his cot. "No, there isn't." He glanced up. "I need to speak with Mr. Lynch, however."

"Indeed. I think Mr. Lynch is some sort of…what is the term? Confident man?"

"Confidence man."

"That's it. For some reason, he wants his daughter—if she is his daughter, not just his partner in crime—married to you, badly enough to stage this whole affair."

"But why? I have nothing! I *am* nothing!"

Andel shook his head. "To be *something* does not always involve owning a great house and lands, or living in a palace for that matter. Surely you know that."

Major sat on his cot and ran his hands through his hair. "I know what you're referring to. Losing Comfort Fields was a blow to my family. Still is."

"Yes, I can see that. But you are not Comfort Fields. You never were."

Major looked at him. "You're right. Perhaps I'd forgotten that."

"And your brothers as well. Perhaps they need the eldest to remind them?"

Major pondered that. "Perhaps. Once 'the eldest' gets it through his own thick skull, of course." He sighed. "Thank you, Andel."

"You are most welcome, Major. Or would you prefer Quince?"

"I'll answer to either. So never mind Denver." Major reached into his pocket and pulled out the money Andel had given him.

But Andel waved it off. "Keep it. Consider it payment if I need further assistance from you."

Major knew at least well enough not to refuse a gift. "Actually, I could use further assistance from you. I'd like to know why Mr. Lynch is doing what he's doing."

"Don't we have a rehearsal to go to?" the giant asked.

"In my view, the rehearsal seems less important."

Andel nodded. "True. I would be happy to help you see to it that justice is served."

"Justice? I don't know that they've actually committed a crime…"

Andel groaned. "Are you blind, Major? Don't you see how they've robbed you already?"

Major blinked, frowned, blinked. "This seems to be my day for discovering my own foolishness. Very well, then—spell it out for me, if you'd be so kind."

Andel laughed. "I shall. But first…" He closed the distance between them, wrapped an arm around Major and crushed him to his side. "…first, Mr. Comfort, allow me to show you how things are done here in Clear Creek."

"Do I have…a…choice?" Major managed.

Andel smiled. "No."

"Somehow I knew…you'd…say that." Andel began to drag him toward the door. "Where are…*gasp*…we going?"

"For this, we're going to need some help."

Chapter Eighteen

Honoria stood off to one side as Annie led the first few songs, followed by the solo and duet performances. The audience was made up of the rest of Clear Creek's residents, including the men from the men's camp. She marveled at the amount of talent in the little town. Some of the performances were astounding—Bowen and Ellie Drake's rendition of "O Holy Night" was otherworldly, and Mr. Mulligan and Mr. Dunnigan managed a surprisingly capable "Good King Wenceslas."

Then it was the children's turn. Honoria waited for the adults to clear the chancel before she started ushering the children into it. The littlest ones were very excited and kept stopping to turn and wave at the audience. "Come now, don't dawdle," she whispered, even as people in the first few pews laughed.

Maddie came to the rescue. "Listen to Miss Cooke, we don't have all day." She touched Honoria on the arm. "Here, I was asked to give you this." She handed her a piece of paper.

"What is it? Who's it from?"

"Read it later—you haven't time now." She dashed off

to the piano, having volunteered to play for the children's numbers.

True enough, Honoria thought, taking a deep breath. It was probably just a note from Mrs. Upton about the refreshment tables—maybe she didn't think they had enough of something. Well, she couldn't worry about it now. She shoved the note inside the pocket of her dress that held her handkerchief, focused on the children fidgeting as they waited for her and gave them a stern yet playful stare.

The children quieted and stood at attention. She raised her hands and gave Maddie a single nod. The opening chords from "Joy to the World" filled the church, and then the children's voices did.

Honoria had never felt so proud. It seemed a small thing to lead them in a few Christmas songs, but at the same time she was an integral part of something new and fun. She'd helped bring it about. In that moment, she realized how much she loved Clear Creek, its people, and most of all, her family.

Two more songs, and her part of the performance was over. The children laughed and giggled with excitement as they exited, Preacher Jo helping them along as mothers came out of pews to gather their own and add them to the audience.

Once the children were settled, Honoria took her seat at the end of the second row on the right, with her aunt, uncle and cousins. Her parents sat in the first with her siblings and the Dunnigans. Uncle Colin leaned over to whisper in her ear. "Well done, poppet. It's not going to be the same around here without you."

She turned away, grimaced, then looked at him. "It's not like I'll never come back."

"You might not if you find a husband."

"If I do, I hope he finds ranch life to his liking."

"Takes a sturdy bloke to live out here," he commented with a grin.

"Shhhh!" Mrs. Dunnigan chastised, turning around to glare at them.

"My apologies," Colin whispered with a brilliant smile that he knew annoyed her.

She scowled at him and turned back just as the piano started playing "Angels We Have Heard on High."

"Oh, I love this one!" Honoria heard her father say.

Honoria smiled and relaxed. She was so used to playing some part in the Christmas play, she'd never had the chance to watch it. She sat, listened, laughed and clapped along with the rest of the townsfolk.

Then she remembered the note tucked into her sleeve. Between songs, she excused herself and went to the refreshment tables at the back of the church. When she got there, everything looked in order, though without the normal amount of lanterns lit it was hard to tell, and Mrs. Upton wasn't there to ask. She didn't want to go looking for her. Finally she decided to just read the note. She pulled it out and held it up toward a lantern to see.

Meet me in the livery stable after your performance.
M.C.

Her heart stopped. Major wanted to meet her in the livery stable? Good grief, what on Earth for?

She quickly glanced around. He probably wanted to talk with her before he left for Denver, but what about? Of course, she wanted to talk to him too. Maybe he figured if they spoke during the concert, they'd have more privacy. She shrugged, then remembered her coat was in the church office. There was no way to get to it without disrupting the performance, so she opted to simply go without. As quietly as she could, she slipped out the church doors and into the crisp night air.

Outsidc was the Platonic ideal of a white Christmas, but she didn't have time to dally. The concert would be over soon and she was supposed to be in charge of the cookie table. She hurried along, admiring the moonlit snow as best she could. She always thought the sight was terribly romantic. She had a fleeting thought of being kissed by Major in the falling snow, the moon glistening off the white snow-covered ground…

…no, that was a fantasy she needed to let go. No doubt they'd say their goodbyes, then he'd head to Denver and she for England. It was time to grow up and leave childish dreams behind.

She entered through the livery's side door and stepped into the work area. It was warmer than she expected. She was half-tempted to give the forge a blast of the bellows to keep it that way.

"Honoria?"

She jumped. He must've arrived just before she did. "Major? Where are you?"

She heard the strike of a match. Major lit a lantern, hung it on a nail pounded into a post and turned to her. "Well, this is rather unusual."

"I daresay." My, but he was handsome, especially in what had to be his Sunday best. She realized that if he was here, he wasn't at the concert. "What are you doing? You're supposed to be singing."

"I should ask the same of you," he replied, coming closer. "I find this all very unusual."

"You do? Then why drag me out of the church to talk here?"

"Drag *you* out? Personally, this could have waited until

after the performance. Mrs. King is going to be very upset with me, and so will my brothers."

"What? Major, you are making absolutely no sense."

He grinned that wonderful grin of his. She hadn't seen it in a long time and forgot how it made her heart flutter. "What exactly is it you require of me, Honoria?"

"Require of you? I don't understand—you asked to meet me here." She pulled the note out of her pocket and waved it.

"My dear lady, *you* asked *me*." He took a piece of paper from his coat pocket and held it out for inspection.

She snatched it from his hand, unfolded it and read:

Meet me in the livery stable after my performance.
H.C.

She gaped at him. "What in… I didn't send this!"

"But if you didn't, then who did?"

"That's what I'd like to know!"

To Honoria's utter horror, Lucretia Lynch stepped into the lamplight and went straight to Major. "If you wanted me alone, you could have just said so. You didn't need to send a note."

Major looked between the two women. "You sent this?" he asked Lucretia.

She snaked an arm around his. "What if I did?" Then she looked at Honoria. "What I want to know is, what is *she* doing here?"

"I came because *he* sent me a note," Honoria said. "Or someone pretending to be him did."

Lucretia glared at him. "Did you?"

Major sighed. "No, though I wished I'd thought of it. I came because someone pretending to be *her* sent me a note."

"Well, no matter," Lucretia replied, missing the hint. "But so long as we're here, why don't we make the most of it?" She nodded at Honoria. "As soon as you leave, of course."

Honoria frowned. The sight of Lucretia latched onto Major was almost more than she could stand, and the urge to find the nearest horse whip and teach the Reb tramp some manners was tempting. But she had to remember why she was there—and staying there. She sighed and stepped closer to the forge for warmth.

"Are you cold?" Major asked. He pried himself from Lucretia and started to take off his coat.

"Only a little," Lucretia said.

Major turned to her, noted the thick coat she wore and rolled his eyes. He finished taking off his own and went to Honoria. "Where's your coat? You'll freeze out here."

"Only if I go outside," she said flatly, then looked over her shoulder. "Which I'm not planning to just yet."

He wrapped his coat around her. "Don't take it off," he whispered, a hand on her shoulder.

She glanced at the hand, then at him. There was that intense stare of his, the one that could make her forget who she was. "What are we doing here, Major?" she said.

His eyes roamed her face, settling on her lips. "I don't know. But…if you'll forgive me being so forward, I'm glad I am."

She could feel the heat coming off his body and trembled at the closeness. "I…shouldn't be here. I need to get back."

The hand on her shoulder moved to her hair. "Do you really have to go?"

She gasped as his fingers found their way into her locks. "Major, what are you…"

"Doing?" he said as his other arm wrapped around her waist.

"Yes! What *are* you doing?" Lucretia huffed.

Major's eyes flicked to her, then locked on Honoria's. "Something I should have done a long time ago." Before either woman could say another word, his lips joined with Honoria's, leaving no doubt in anyone's mind exactly what he was doing.

"Why, I never!" Lucretia screeched. "How…how…"

"Scandalous?"

Honoria squeaked in alarm against Major's mouth as she recognized the voice. Andel Berg? Why was *he* here?

Major broke the kiss slowly, tenderly, and gazed into her eyes in the dim lamplight. "Honoria, I'm so sorry."

She swallowed hard, not understanding. "For what?"

"For not doing that sooner."

Lucretia groaned in disgust. "Oh for Heaven's sake!"

"Indeed," Mr. Berg said in all seriousness. "This behavior can't be tolerated!"

Honoria, her mind still in a kiss induced fog, finally gave the giant her attention. "What?"

"You, young lady, have been compromised!" he pointed a long finger at her.

Honoria blanched. "What?!"

Mr. Berg spun to Lucretia. "Run for the preacher!"

"I'll do no such thing! It's obvious this was all planned!"

"Really?" Mr. Berg said in innocence. "How can you tell?"

"Because, er… I…" She turned to Major. "Why did you ask me here? What was this note all about? And why is she here?"

"In order: I didn't. I don't know what note you mean. And while I don't know why she's here, I'm glad she is—and I wish you weren't."

"This is ridiculous!" Lucretia hissed. "Wait until my father hears about this!"

"He already has," Mr. Berg said, taking out his pocket watch and flipping it open.

No sooner had he done so than Mr. Lynch burst through the doors at the other end of the stable. "Lucretia! What has he done to you! Someone call for the preacher!"

Major moved in front of Honoria as if to protect her from the newcomer.

Mr. Berg smiled. "My thoughts exactly. He should come right away and see to this whole nasty business."

Mr. Lynch pointed a finger at Major. "I demand you make things right by my daughter."

Major stepped away from Honoria and raised a single eyebrow. "Your daughter?"

"That's right! You'd better do the right thing!" He turned to Mr. Berg. "Were you a witness? Did you see what happened?"

Mr. Berg gave him the tiniest hint of a smile. "Indeed, sir, I did."

"That settles it, then! She was compromised, wasn't she?" Mr. Lynch went on.

"One could say that." Mr. Berg calmly turned toward the nearest door.

"Fetch that preacher!" Mr. Lynch cried. "There's not a moment to lose!" He pulled a gun and aimed it at Major.

"Whoa!" Major placed himself in front of Honoria again. "There's no need for that."

"You'd better make sure he stays put," Mr. Berg told Mr. Lynch. "We'll go fetch what's needed."

Lucretia rolled her eyes. "Daddy! Don't you see what's...?"

"Come along, Miss Lynch," Mr. Berg said, grabbing her arm and pulling her toward the door.

"Unhand me, you brute!"

"Now, now, Miss Lynch. You don't want to see your father have to shoot Mr. Comfort."

"Shoot him? Why…" But Mr. Berg hurried her out the door before she could finish.

Mr. Lynch cackled. "Now we'll set things to rights, you…you scoundrel!"

Honoria, her wits returning, glanced between the two men. "Huh?"

Major eyed the gun in the other man's hand, then looked back at Honoria. "It's all right. Everything's all right."

"Everything is…well, confusing at the moment," she said, her mind still on his kiss.

"Things will all be made clear, trust me."

"I don't…that…hmmm…" A memory began surfacing in her mind. Could it be? If so, the next thing to happen would be…

Sure enough, people started filing into the stable—including her parents. Honoria's father took one look at Major obviously protecting her and gasped. "What are you two doing in here?"

She peeked around Major's shoulder at him. "Frankly, Papa, I think you're about to find out." Then she began to giggle.

"What's so funny?" Major hissed back at her, then finally turned around, ignoring Mr. Lynch's weapon. "Care to explain it to me?"

"In a minute I won't have to," she replied, still giggling. She knew how this story went—she'd heard it before, many times. *Oh, Andel Berg, you stinker!* "Please don't go to Denver. And please, please don't marry that Lynch woman."

"Honoria, I wasn't going to do either. As far as Miss Lynch, I never was."

She stopped laughing and gaped. "You weren't?"

"Not in a million years." Major sighed and, ignoring the gasps of the onlookers, pulled her close. "Honoria Cooke, it seems we've had a misunderstanding."

"It seems we have."

"Unhand her, you blackguard!" Harrison yelled above the crowd.

Now Honoria had a wicked grin on her face. "It's too late, Papa—the blackguard corrupted me when he kissed me!"

"Kissed you?!" Harrison said, his voice cracking. Several of the townsfolk expressed outrage—or delight.

Major rested his cheek against her head. "Oh Honoria—please, please don't go to England. Stay here."

"I'd need a very good reason to stay."

"There's every reason if we're to be married," he replied.

The stable went silent, despite more and more people making their way in. Harrison's mouth slowly fell open. "What did you say, sir?"

"Oh, you heard him clear as a bell," Sadie replied, having finally caught up with her husband. She was smiling hugely, and Honoria knew she had gotten the idea too.

Before Harrison could answer her, Mr. Berg shoved his way through the crowd, pushing a flustered Rev. Josiah King in front of him. "There—there's the culprit! You know what to do!"

Preacher Jo glanced up at Mr. Berg, who winked. "My, my, Andel, but this seems oddly familiar." He looked at Major and Honoria. "The livery stable is becoming a popular place for this sort of thing."

Major was still confused. "What is going on?"

Honoria started giggling again.

"It seems you're getting married," Preacher Jo said.

"At least this time it's not in the middle of my supper." He glared at Mr. Berg again. "Though I certainly would've preferred it hadn't disrupted the Christmas singing. Right in the middle of 'Silent Night,' ironically enough..."

Mr. Lynch snorted in disgust. "What are you all talking about? This man compromised my daughter! I demand he marry her!"

"*Your* daughter?" Preacher Jo said in surprise. "By all accounts, he's compromised Miss Cooke here."

Harrison screeched, tried to move forward through the crowd—and almost fell over due to Sadie's hammer-lock on his arm. "Unhand me, wife!"

"Can someone get me a rope?" Sadie asked. Several townsfolk laughed as a furious but embarrassed Harrison subsided.

Mr. Lynch started to wave his gun around. "You people are all witnesses!"

"Sure we are," Mr. Dunnigan called as he wormed his way to the front. "Wouldn't miss it for the world."

Mr. Lynch smiled and nodded in triumph, not grasping that his daughter was nowhere in sight. "Let's get on with it, then!"

"Ye heard the man, Preacher Jo," Mrs. Mulligan called out. "Get on with it."

"Oh very well, but then it's back to the church before the children eat all the cookies!" More laughter.

Honoria looked at Major, who still didn't seem to be catching on. Did he know the story of the Bergs' wedding? Probably not—she'd have to tell him later. "Were you serious about wanting to marry me?"

"Absolutely."

"Well, no time like the present."

Major grinned that grin.

Mr. Lynch blanched. "What's this?"

A huge hand grabbed his shoulder. It was one of the Bergs' guards, quite tall and broad, with his face hidden by a plaid scarf. "Take Mr. Lynch to his daughter, will you?" Mr. Berg instructed. "You'll find her in the church office being entertained by Mr. Kiggins and some of the children."

"What?!" Mr. Lynch cried. "What are you doing? Let go of me! My daughter is supposed to be marrying this man! It was all arrang…er… I mean…"

Mr. Berg stopped the guard holding poor Lynch and bent to his ear. "Mr. Lynch, I think you should probably stop talking."

"Afore ya incriminate yerself," Sheriff Tom Turner clarified. "His Highness informed me of yer shenanigans."

"But perhaps," Mr. Berg continued, "you and I can meet later over some *pie* and discuss it." He turned to his men. "Take him away."

As Mr. Lynch was hauled off, even Irene Dunnigan looked impressed. "Now that there is how a king acts."

"Prince consort," five people corrected—including Mr. Berg.

Preacher Jo glanced around before turning to Honoria and Major. "Tell me, do the two of you really want to get married in *here*?"

Major continued to hold Honoria close. "It hardly seems dignified to wed in a stable."

Honoria looked up. "Major dear, since when do I care about dignity? Besides, it was good enough for the future queen and prince consort of Dalrovia, so it's good enough for me."

"But…"

"My daughter…" Harrison declared, then swallowed hard. "…can get married wherever she pleases."

She pulled away from Major and ran into her father's arms. "Oh Papa, thank you!"

"It seems you're bound and determined, sweetling. I might as well let you have your head and see what transpires."

"You won't be sorry, Papa, I promise."

Major watched the two and smiled. He glanced over at Mr. Berg. "So what did you find out about Archibald Lynch?"

"For one, that it may not be his real name," Mr. Berg replied. "It seems he's a busy man, and probably a wanted one. Sheriff Turner and I hope to find out over pie."

"But why was he picking on Major?" Honoria asked, returning to her now-fiancé's embrace.

"We think he was under the impression the Comforts were still in possession of their titular plantation, and thus their fortune," Mr. Berg explained. "It's the only logical explanation."

"But as we all know, I've nothing to offer a wife in that respect," Major said. "All I do have is my honor, my integrity, a willing heart, my fear of the good Lord and these two hands. If you'll have them."

Honoria smiled. "Yes, yes I will!"

"About time," Wilfred breathed a sigh of relief.

"Now that that's settled, let's get back to the church," Preacher Jo said.

"To marry us?" Honoria asked.

"No, because I'm hungry. You can get married later!"

Honoria sighed. "Well, at least I won't have to stand on a bucket..." Everyone—even Major, though he didn't get the joke—laughed as they headed out into the night.

Epilogue

Christmas Day, 1877

"Do you, Honoria Alexandra Cooke, take this man to be your lawfully wedded husband?" Preacher Jo asked. It had been decided the night before that Major and Honoria should be married the next day, and the couple had agreed to it.

Honoria was wearing her mother's wedding dress, her aunt's veil and couldn't have looked lovelier. She opened her mouth to speak, then turned and looked at her parents in the first pew. Harrison met her gaze, tears streaming down his face. She smiled and turned back to Major. "I do."

"And do you, Major Quincy Comfort, take this woman to be your lawfully wedded wife?"

Major was decked in a suit loaned to him by Colin Cooke. Though out of fashion, Honoria thought it made her new husband the handsomest man on Earth. He smiled as well, glanced at his brothers and back, then said, "I most certainly do."

"Then by the power vested in me by Almighty God and the state of Oregon, I now pronounce you man and wife!"

An unfamiliar wail sounded from the back of the

church. All heads turned as Mr. Berg's guard, the one with the plaid scarf, whipped a handkerchief out of some hidden fold of his Dalrovian cloak and blew his nose.

Preacher Jo stared at him a moment, shrugged and got back to work. "Mr. Comfort, you may kiss the bride."

Major lifted the veil from Honoria's face. "Don't mind if I do," he said, took her in his arms and kissed her soundly.

"Ohhhh," came a loud sigh from the back.

Preacher Jo rubbed a hand over his face. "Who *is* that?"

Major glanced at the back of the church. "I have no idea, but he's certainly…vocal." He drew Honoria closer. "I say we give him something to remember." Before she could protest, he tipped her backward and kissed her again.

"Oh! Ohhhh my!"

At this point no one knew where to look: at Major and Honoria, or the cloaked dramatist in the back. Mr. Berg, at this point, was looking as perturbed as Preacher Jo.

Thankfully Major broke the kiss and faced the congregation. Everyone cheered as the couple started down the center aisle, headed for the Christmas supper with all the trimmings being held at the hotel.

"I say, Andel, but where are the Lynches?" Colin asked as they stood to follow the happy couple out of the church.

"Mr. Lynch wasn't feeling well this morning," Andel explained.

Maddie slapped him on the arm. "No thanks to you."

"It was only twelve pies," Tom Turner said in their defense.

"Good heavens!" Colin laughed. "I'd forgotten all about that! You made the man eat *twelve* pies?"

"Aw, heavens no. He only ate three 'fore he spilled everythin'."

"Everything?" Harrison said.

"Yes." Andel replied flatly. "Some of it on Sheriff Turner's boots."

"Egads," Colin said as he left the pew. "Say no more."

Tom shrugged. "I've dealt with worse."

"I will say this," Andel continued. "We were right. He's wanted in several states for forgery, embezzlement and fraud."

"A confidence man?" Harrison said in wonder.

"And his daughter?" Belle asked as she followed them down the aisle.

"That there's the sad part," Tom said. "The only thin' she's guilty of is bein' shallow and spoiled. And in one case, a li'l too trustin'."

"Too trusting?" Sadie asked as they went outside. "What do you mean?"

The Bergs' royal guard closed in around them, the tallest one still sniffing into his handkerchief now and then. Andel sighed sadly and turned to Sadie. "She's with child."

"What?" the Cookes said at once.

"Yep," Tom confirmed. "She needed to marry for the youngun's sake. She ain't got any real money to speak of, and neither does her pa. He was hopin' she'd marry someone rich to secure his own future—I don't think he cared much about hers."

"That poor woman," Belle commented as her eyes sought the hotel. "Are they going to stay in town?"

"In a jail cell, you mean," said Sadie.

"Since Mr. Lynch crossed state lines, he's what ya'd call a federal case," Tom explained. "Tomorrow Eli's gonna go to the nearest telegraph office and wire the state pen in Salem to send a U.S. marshal out for him. He won't be givin' Clear Creek no more trouble."

"But what about poor Miss Lynch?" Harrison asked.

"I wouldn't worry about her," Andel told him. "It seems Jasper Kiggins from the men's camp is quite taken with her. I've given Mr. Van Cleet enough money to cover her room at the hotel long enough for Jasper to court her—at least until spring, when he plans to leave."

"I've heard mention of him going to Astoria," Colin said. "Good man, Jasper."

"Indeed, he is. Maddie and I will speak to Miss Lynch personally about her predicament. It's too bad about her father, but I'm afraid he'd only try to manipulate her condition further if allowed to stay."

"Your Royal Highness?" the guard with the plaid said in a sing-song voice. The Cookes' stared at him, wondering what his story was. Only his steel grey eyes could be seen. The rest of him was hidden by the plaid wrapped around his head, lower face and neck.

"Yes?" Andel said.

"All is ready."

"Very well. Rest until I have need of you."

The guard bowed, straightened, then turned gracefully and left.

"Andel," Harrison said. "Who is that? I've not seen him around until last night."

"A…representative from the court, you might say. He's been delayed in joining us."

"Certainly an odd fellow," Colin said. "I swear he cried through half the wedding."

Andel and Maddie laughed. "Mr. Melvale can be quite emotional at times," Maddie agreed. "He's flamboyant, I'll grant, but he'd lay his life down for us if he had to."

Andel watched Melvale head for the hotel. "And so he has." He turned to the others. "But that's a story for another time. Now we celebrate the marriage of Harrison's daughter to Mr. Comfort, a man I'm quite impressed with. He has everything Honoria needs. They are a good match."

Harrison nodded. "I feel like a fool for not seeing it before." He offered a hand to his longtime friend. "Thank you, Andel, for seeing it for me."

Andel took his hand and pulled Harrison into a crushing embrace, slapping him on the back. "You're welcome." He stepped back. "You all did the same for me once, and now I'm married to the most beautiful woman in the world."

Maddie blushed. "Despite the massive firepower involved at our wedding?"

"True, but I'd have married you even without the whole town waving arms in my face."

Everyone laughed at that. "We're going to miss the two of you when you leave," Colin said. "Do you really have to go?"

"I'm afraid so," said Andel. "Besides a country to run, we need to get back to our children. But we'll try to come back when they're a little older. In the meantime, you've got quite a task on your hands."

"What's that?"

Andel grinned. "Major Comfort has five unmarried brothers."

"That, dear fellow, is Major's problem," Harrison pointed out.

"But your wife is so good at matchmaking, perhaps she could lend a hand?"

"Oh no," Sadie said. "I'm retired from that, thanks. Best leave it to the professionals."

"Like Mrs. Pettigrew?" Maddie asked with a laugh as they continued into the hotel.

"Exactly!" Sadie agreed.

Inside, the townsfolk were already eating, the music was playing (specifically Henry Fig, the only one who remembered to bring an instrument) and children were everywhere. Not only was it Major and Honoria's wedding, but Christmas, and many had brought their gifts from home to open at the wedding supper.

Honoria saw her family and hurried over. "Papa! Did you see the cake?"

"No, sweetling, not yet. Show me."

Honoria grabbed him by the hand and was off.

Colin laughed. "I hope Major can handle her."

Sadie laughed too. "I hope *she* can handle *him*. He won't put up with her nonsense, I can tell."

"Then they really are a good match," Belle confirmed.

"That they are," Andel agreed. "Now let's go take a look at that cake." And the others followed the royal family of Dalrovia into the hotel dining room.

Only in Clear Creek.

* * * * *

If you enjoyed Dear Mr. Comfort, *then be watching for* Dear Mr. Vander. *We'll travel to Independence, Oregon, where you'll get to visit with some of your favorite characters from past books of mine. And speaking of books, if you're not familiar with the Bergs' story, you can find them in the series that started it all: Prairie Brides, where you can read about Sadie and Belle's own adventures with their future husbands, Harrison and Colin, not to mention their brother Duncan, the duke. Andel and Maddie's story is told in* Her Prairie Viking *(Prairie Brides, Book Four).*
Check out the Prairie Bride Series here:
http://www.authorkitmorgan.com/prairie-brides/
You'll be glad you did!
All of Kit Morgan's books can be found at her website www.authorkitmorgan.com. Be sure to sign up for Kit's newsletter to learn more about upcoming books and special surprises!

About the Author

Kit Morgan, aka Geralyn Beauchamp, lives in a log cabin in the woods in the wonderful state of Oregon. She grew up riding horses, playing cowboys and Indians and has always had a love of Westerns! She and her father watched many Western movies and television shows together, and enjoyed the quirky characters of *Green Acres*. Kit's books have been described as "*Green Acres* meets *Gunsmoke*," and have brought joy and entertainment to thousands of readers. Many of her books are now in audio format, performed by a talented voice actor who brings Kit's characters to life, and can be found on Amazon, Audible.com and iTunes.